A. FRANK SMITH, JR. LIBRARY CENTER
SOUTHWESTERN UNIVERSITY
GEORGETOWN, TEXAS

WITHDRAWN

A. FRANK SMITH, JR. LIBRARY CENTER
WESTERN UNIVERSITY

DATE DUE

FACULTY ITEM DUE END OF SPRING SEMESTER			

Demco No. 62-0549

A FAMILY PROJECT

A FAMILY PROJECT

Sarah Ellis

Margaret K. McElderry Books

NEW YORK

First published in Canada 1986
by Douglas & McIntyre/Groundwood Books, Vancouver/Toronto

Copyright © 1986 by Sarah Ellis

All rights reserved. No part of this book may be reproduced or transmitted
in any form or by any means, electronic or mechanical, including
photocopying, recording, or by any information storage and retrieval
system, without permission in writing from the Publisher.

Margaret K. McElderry Books
Macmillan Publishing Company
866 Third Avenue
New York, NY 10022

Composition by Maryland Linotype Composition Company
Baltimore, Maryland

Designed by Barbara A. Fitzsimmons

First United States Edition 1988

Printed in the United States of America

10 9 8 7 6 5 4 3 2

Library of Congress Cataloging-in-Publication Data

Ellis, Sarah.
The family project.

Previously published as: The baby project.
Summary: Excited by the unexpected prospect of a
baby, eleven-year-old Jessica and her family eagerly
prepare for the changes the new arrival will bring to
their lives.
[1. Babies—Fiction.   2. Family life—Fiction.
3. Family problems—Fiction.   4. Death—Fiction]
I. Title.
PZ7.E4758Fam   1988   [Fic]   87-22818
ISBN 0-689-50444-6

This novel is a work of fiction. Names, characters, places and
incidents are either the product of the author's imagination or are used
fictitiously. Any resemblance to actual persons, living or dead, events
or locales is entirely coincidental.

CF
El 58l

For the Seymour family,
who are part of this book
in so many ways,
and especially for Julia Lynn.

1

*J*essica leaned against the kitchen counter and watched her dad roll out cookies.

"Hey, Dad, listen to this. We have one zero one people in our family. Get it?"

"Well, it sure feels like a hundred and one on laundry day."

"No, I mean really. That's how big our family is in base two. Do you know about base two?"

"Sure. Second base, right behind the pitcher."

"Come on, Dad, this is math, not baseball. Didn't you learn about base two in school?"

"I think I had chicken pox that day."

"Well, look, I'll show you." Jessica grabbed a piece of cookie dough and molded five blobs. "Okay, here's our family—you, Mum, Rowan, Simon and me. Now let's put us into sets of two. You and Mum, one set. Rowan and Simon, one set. Me, left over. Now, draw a ring around each of the pairs."

Dad hesitated. "What about Ollie and Lavinia?"

"Dad, forget the cat and the computer. Just do it."

Dad drew two rings in the floury board.

"Is that it?" Jessica asked with a grin.

"Think so."

"Ha! You missed the pair of pairs." Jessica drew a ring around Mum, Dad, Rowan and Simon. "Look, there's one by itself. That's one in the ones column. There aren't any pairs by themselves. That's zero in the pairs column. And one pair of pairs, that's one in the pairs of pairs column. One, zero, one. Right?"

"Isn't it time for recess yet?" said Dad.

Jessica ignored him. "But don't you think it's fun? You can have base anything, but computers use two. We learned it at school today. Can I have this?" Jessica grabbed her dough family and squished them into a lump.

"Hold it, Jess. What would six be?"

Jessica was surprised. Was Dad really *interested* in base two? She had really only brought it up for something to say. She thought for a minute. "One, one, zero," she announced.

"A hundred and ten," said Dad. "Think of it." Then he got his faraway look that always meant the end of a conversation, so Jessica grabbed her jacket and took the cookie dough out to the back porch.

A FAMILY PROJECT

It was the first non-rainy day they had had all February, and Jessica wanted to be outside, shivery or not. She looked down to the water, to the narrow view of mountains and bay framed on either side by buildings. A sailboat appeared from one side of the picture and sailed off the other side. Jessica rolled bits of dough between her fingers, popped them into her mouth and played an old game. The highrise apartment she collapsed in a local earthquake. The green house she burnt to the ground. The condominium she caught in a large net and let the eagles carry it away. And when the dust and the smoke cleared and the eagles were a spot in the distance, Jessica on her porch could see the whole bay, with black freighters heading for the harbor and the snow-hatted mountains behind.

She was chewing the last dough blob when Charlene the tenant sputtered down the side path on her moped.

"Jess, just the person I wanted to see. Come on down, quick. I've got this great new hair stuff and I need a model."

Charlene lived in the basement and was the fifth tenant the Robertsons had had. As far as Jessica was concerned, she was the best. She worked at a beauty salon doing make-up and manicures, but her real interest was country and western music. "Look, Jess," she would say, "I know that I can't make much money writing songs at first, so I'm going to open a make-up salon and then get people to work for me and then I can spend my time more creatively."

Charlene was always sending her songs away to famous

singers, but so far none had responded. The Robertson family heard a lot of the songs as the sounds drifted up the hot-air register. "Better than Brussels sprouts," Dad always said, recalling the last tenant but one who did late-night cooking.

Before Charlene, the Brussels sprouts eater and the other tenants were mostly people not to bother. "Don't bounce balls or skip in the kitchen." "Don't use up all the hot water." "Don't stare in the basement window as you walk down the side path."

But Charlene really seemed to enjoy Jessica's company. Charlene was the only grown-up Jessica had ever met who actually talked to her like an equal. Jessica had figured out that there were lots of ways that adults talked to children. The most obnoxious way was Uncle Gordie's. His idea of a conversation opener was, "So, got any boyfriends yet?" And then whatever you replied, Uncle Gordie would say, "Quite the little gal you've got there, Dave," to Jessica's dad. Jessica's best friend Margaret said there was only one answer to questions like that, and it was, "Why on earth would you ask such a personal question?" But Jessica had never had the courage to say it. It sounded too lippy. "If adults are rude to children there's no reason why children have to take it," said Margaret. But then again, Margaret got into a lot more trouble than Jessica ever wanted to.

Mum on the other hand, wasn't obnoxious, but she still talked to kids in a special way. It was as though her words were printed in capital letters. Because she was at work such long hours on school days, she always tried to have QUALITY TIME with Jessica on weekends. Time for IMPORTANT CONVERSATIONS.

Jessica could usually predict what the topic would be. Mum read lots of articles on parenting and she usually left them in the bathroom. Friday night Jessica would lie in the bathtub reading. "Your Child and Advertising: Raising a Conscious Consumer." Sure enough, on Saturday morning Mum would say, "Isn't it INTERESTING how we buy Puffo-buds for breakfast. I WONDER how we DECIDE to buy them instead of some other cereal." Jessica's brother Simon had taken to escaping this quality time by wearing his Walkman to breakfast.

Dad was completely different. He just kidded and fooled around. A conversation with him was like a badminton game, trying to keep the bird in the air—"Wouldn't it be funny if . . . WHAP. Yeah, but it would be worse if . . . WHAP. But what about . . . WHAP." It was fun, but Jessica knew that Dad gave her easy shots to return.

Conversation with Charlene was much easier. She wasn't obnoxious or cute or patient. And you didn't need to be smart or funny in return. Charlene talked to Jessica as though Jessica were nineteen, not eleven. Maybe that was because Charlene's conversation was mostly about Charlene. Jessica knew about every boyfriend ("He's gorgeous but, you know, not centered."), about Charlene's family who lived in the country ("They just don't, like, sympathize with my lifestyle.") and all about the people that

5

Charlene worked with—which one was going to leave her husband while the going was good, which one had just bought a condo, which one was taking the Escapaventure Tour to Reno. Today, though, Charlene didn't have a story. She got right to work on Jessica's head.

The great new hair stuff turned out to be a sort of metallic jelly. First Charlene wet Jessica's hair, then toweled it dry. Then she applied the jelly all over her hair. It felt like an aerial attack of killer slime. But the very weirdest part was when Charlene vacuumed Jessica's head to make all the hair stand up in spikes. The color was blue. Jessica's head felt very tight. She looked like a sea urchin. Jessica kept touching the spiky ends with her fingertips.

"Hey, Jess, it looks excellent. Your fine pale hair is perfect for this gel."

Jessica thought how much better "fine, pale" sounded than "thin, beige."

Charlene made a few final adjustments. "Say, how's Rowan doing these days, now that he's out there on his own?"

Jessica's oldest brother had moved out in January to his own place.

"Okay, I guess. I went to visit him. He keeps his knives and forks in a bag."

"What?"

"He has this bag that hangs on the kitchen wall. All his cutlery lives in it. He keeps everything in bags—his Kleenex, his records. Even his bed goes into a bag in the morning."

"Weird. How come?"

"Well, he bought this big sewing machine and all this material and zippers and stuff and he's going to make bags for skis and tennis racquets and sports things. He even has a business card. It says, 'Rowan Robertson, the Bagman.' Underneath it says, 'a bag for everything and everything in its bag.' "

"So, do you like his place?"

"It's okay. It's very tidy." Jessica was still a bit mad at Rowan for leaving. She knew he had hated sharing a room with slobby Simon, but it made a hole in the family. She still set five places at dinner by mistake.

"Is he, like, seeing anyone?"

"You mean a girlfriend?"

"Yeah."

"I don't know. He doesn't say very much."

"That's because he's deep. I like that in a man. Depth. Anyway, how about a Coke?"

That was another great thing about Charlene. She ate junk food. The Robertsons didn't go in for junk too much. It wasn't that they ate all that healthy soy and grains stuff like Cherry Dorkley's family. It was just that Dad always thought you could make nicer treats from scratch.

"Kool-Aid?" he would answer in the summer. "No, c'mon. Let's make old-fashioned lemonade."

And so before you knew it pots of sugar syrup were boiling on the stove and lemons and limes were being squeezed and it had turned into a big production and not really what you had wanted. Charlene was a relief.

They sat drinking Coke from the can and watching "Tomorrow Brings Another Dawn" on TV. "Junk for the body, junk for the mind," said Charlene in a contented way.

That night at dinner, Jessica was a hit with her sea-urchin hair. But after everyone had commented on it, conversation seemed to come to a dead halt. That was happening a lot lately and Jessica didn't know why. She re-arranged her peas and thought of bringing up base two again. But there didn't seem much point. Mum would pretend to be interested. "Fostering self-confidence in your children" was the latest article sitting on the clothes hamper in the bathroom. But she would only be pretending. Base two wouldn't be news to her. She was an engineer and knew all about math and computers. She knew all about everything.

Suddenly Jessica felt tired. She didn't want to be a kid anymore. She wanted to be a grown-up right away. Grown-ups got to be just what they were—jokey or serious or ob-noxious or weird. But kids always had to be what someone expected. It was like being a piece of play dough. The thought of being bright blue and squishy made Jessica feel better.

She looked over at Simon who was eating his fifth cab-bage roll in one enormous bite. No point talking to him about base two or feeling like play dough. He wouldn't even listen. These days he wore his Walkman to dinner as well as breakfast and didn't ever want to play. Maybe she didn't want to grow up after all. If being fourteen meant you didn't want to play, then she didn't ever want to be fourteen. She would stay eleven forever. First she'd be eleven in base ten, then she'd be eleven in base nine, then . . .

"Jessica, *please*," Dad's voice filtered through. "Could you pay some attention to eating? Dinner with this family is getting to be like eating with an order of silent monks, what with Mr. Wired-for-Sound over there and a daughter who is trying to find the answer to the universe in her peas. We could have a little conversation, you know. Some families *share* things at dinner. Some families discuss world affairs. We could even assign a topic if nothing leaped to mind. How about gerbils? You, the youth of today, could share a fresh modern perspective on gerbils. We, the older generation, could share experiences of gerbils of the past. I, for example, could tell you about my career as a door-to-door gerbil salesman. . . ."

"Were you really . . ." Jessica caught herself just in time. No, of course he hadn't really sold gerbils. Believing that would mean she was gullible. With two older brothers you had to be really careful not to be gullible. But sometimes Jessica forgot. Like the time she believed Rowan and Simon telling her that if you could touch the tip of your nose with your tongue, you were descended from royalty. She spread that story all through third grade before she found out the truth.

9

Of course, believing that Dad had actually been a gerbil salesman was a bit different. After all, Dad had been a lot of things—a driving teacher, a gardener, an automatic garage door installer and a tennis court refinisher. Now he was a taxi driver, but not very often.

Dad was still talking. "Your mother could talk about the computer applications of gerbils and then we could share some heartwarming stories of the gerbils we had when we were first married." Then Dad gave Mum a soppy look. He was doing this more and more lately and Jessica found it very embarrassing.

"Simon, perhaps you could research the international scene on gerbils."

By this time Jessica was giggling and Mum had her "family joke" smile on, which meant that she was glad everyone was having a good time so that she could think about her latest engineering problem. But Simon just turned up the volume on his cassette and looked disgusted. Suddenly Jessica missed Rowan so much. Rowan jumped right into conversations like this. Why did he have to move out? Leaving messages on his "Bagman" answering machine was fun, but it wasn't the same as having him around to pretend to crack an egg on your head, to lend you his protractor to draw circles with, to sing ads from TV.

And it wasn't just Rowan leaving. What had happened to Simon? He used to be friendly and call her "squirt." Now they didn't even have good fights. Starting a conversation with him was like talking to a stranger. And what with Mum and Dad acting weird and changing the topic when she came into the room, Jessica was fed up.

Why do things have to *change* all the time, she said to herself. Then she suddenly mashed all her peas into her potatoes. "Base green mush," she whispered.

2

*J*essica woke the next morning to the thunk of the shower being turned on. Quarter to seven. Mum was back from her run. Jessica slid down the bed, hooked her feet over the end, and thought about getting up. But it didn't really work to talk to Mum in the mornings. Jessica liked the halfway feeling of sitting around in her pajamas with sleep in her eyes, sipping cocoa, and letting the day sneak up. Mum was crisp and fast in the mornings. And impatient. Up, run, shower, dress, have a blender breakfast, go away. It was usually better to wait until she had left, even if it did mean fighting for the shower.

Downstairs the air was jangly. Dad was being firm with Simon. "Simon, I want you home for dinner tonight. Six o'clock. Don't make other plans. We're having a family meeting."

"Thought we'd given those up," said Simon, inhaling his usual mixing bowl full of cereal.

Jessica spread peanut butter on her toast. It wasn't good news. Family meetings usually meant Mum talking a lot in capitals and then the whole family getting involved in some project that left everything in a mess until they gradually forgot about it. Like the Christmas they drew lots to see who gave gifts to whom and somehow Simon got left out and Dad had to rush downtown at five o'clock on Christmas Eve to try to find him a "Planet of the Apes" kite.

"Earth to Jessica, earth to Jessica." Her dad's voice reached her. "Jessica, please, can you get on with your toast? And did you hear what I said to Simon? Dinner at six, sharp."

"What's the meeting about, anyway?" asked Simon.

Dad turned from the sink with a half-smile. "All will be revealed in the fullness of time."

Jessica buzzed the intercom at Margaret's apartment on her way to school. "Pizza delivery for Miss Lee." Margaret buzzed her into the lobby and Jessica read the names on all the mailboxes before Margaret emerged from the elevator.

"Family conference tonight," said Jessica, "but I can't figure out what for. Dad didn't seem mad or anything, just kind of twinkly. I'll phone you as soon as I find out about it."

Over the day Jessica forgot about the meeting. For one

thing, Mr. Blackburn announced a new project. Mr. Blackburn was very big on projects. Jessica sometimes wished he would just tell them stuff, but they were supposed to learn by doing. Mr. Blackburn learned that in teacher-training school, along with how to use the overhead projector. He was great at the overhead projector.

"I'd like you to form dyads." That was what Mr. Blackburn said for finding a partner. Jessica gave a quick glance at Margaret. The glance was returned. That was okay, then. Once Jessica hadn't been fast enough and Lisa had picked Margaret for a partner, leaving Jessica at the mercy of bossy Lynette, who always wanted to do all the stencil lettering herself.

"I want you to choose an animal and research it, using a variety of media." Jessica sighed. Oh, no. That meant Mr. Blackburn wanted you to go to the school library and look at filmstrips.

"You can present your information in any way you like —essay, model, oral report, set of diagrams or drawings or whatever. Today we'll get together for a first discussion. The dyads can now move together."

A thunder of moving desks made Mr. Blackburn realize he had made a mistake. "No, no. I meant you can move your place to be near your partner. You don't need to push your desks around. Eddie, put your desk right back where it was. There's no need to be silly about this."

Mr. Blackburn was always telling them that there was no need to be silly when, of course, on a Friday afternoon you did have to be silly. The only person who didn't need to be silly on Friday afternoons was Cherry Dorkley, the best-behaved girl in the world.

"So what do you want to do?" asked Margaret.

"I don't know. I sort of like horses."

"*Everybody's* going to do horses. We need something different."

"How about slugs?"

Margaret's eyes lit up. "Hey, great! We could do original research in your garden. We could trace their slime paths and do maps. We could . . ."

"Margaret, forget it. I was only kidding. I *hate* slugs. I don't want to know more about them than I do now."

"Oh, all right." Margaret chewed her eraser. "I've got it. Let's do the duck-billed platypus."

"Okay. But why?"

"Because if we do an essay, every time we write 'duck-billed platypus' we'll use up three words. We won't have to write as much." So the duck-billed platypus it was.

Everyone else picked more or less what you would expect. Cherry Dorkley picked horses. "Told you so," whispered Margaret. Lynette and Lisa picked the panda. "We're very interested in endangered species," said Lynette. Lisa looked as though it were the first time she'd heard of this special interest. Eddie Ramponi and his best friend Doug picked the shark, as did four other male dyads. Mr. Blackburn had to persuade Stephen and Harjinder to change to the shrew by telling them it was the most bloodthirsty creature in the animal kingdom. And then, finally, it was three o'clock.

On the way home, Jessica and Margaret discussed the project. "Cinchy," said Margaret. "Copy a bunch of stuff out of the encyclopedia, then cut out some pictures of Australia from your *National Geographics*. Three hours work, max."

Jessica thought again of how glad she was to have Margaret for a friend. They were a good team. Margaret always had ideas, but she never had any stuff. Her apartment was too small and her mum never let her keep anything. Jessica only had pretty ordinary ideas, but you could find almost anything in her messy house.

Except a quiet place, she thought, as she came in the kitchen door.

Dad was in the kitchen with cookbooks spread all over the table and groceries all over the counters.

"No proper feta cheese in Safeway. Only canned. Safeway has a moral obligation to its customers to have proper feta. Ah, Jessica, would you run over to that Greek grocery and get me half a pound? You know the kind, in brine."

So it was going to be one of those kinds of dinners. Jessica thought that all feta tasted pretty much the same, but you couldn't tell that to Dad. Anyway, she was just as glad to have an errand.

On the way to the Greek grocery, Jessica dropped in at the drugstore to check over the new stock of felt pens. She wondered if allowances were to be on the agenda for the family meeting. Her allowance wasn't stretching too far these days.

She arrived home just as Rowan turned up with a bottle of wine in a black nylon insulated bag. "Newest invention," he announced. "This bag is going to revolutionize picnics, transform barbecues. Every trendy person going to a party is going to want one." He broke an imaginary egg over Jessica's head. "Family confab, I hear."

At six Simon still wasn't home, and Dad was waiting to stir the egg into the egg-lemon soup. The crashing from the kitchen was just starting to get loud when it was matched by a crash from the front door. Simon exploded in and threw his gym bag up the stairs in a mighty heave. This was followed by a loud, "Sorry I'm late," muffled by the closing of the bathroom door. Sounds of a killer whale amusing the aquarium audience emerged. Jessica wondered why boys always exhaled while washing their faces, snorting and bubbling.

During dinner nobody mentioned the meeting, and Mum and Dad were very quiet. All through soup and moussaka and Greek salad, Rowan told a complicated story of how he had figured out a way to make a bag that would turn into a cushion and an umbrella, making it ideal for the football fan.

Finally, over dessert in the living room, Dad cleared his throat in an attention-getting way and said, "Well, now to the business of the evening." He looked very nervous and Jessica wondered for a moment if the Robertsons were about to become a broken home, but surely Mum wouldn't be looking so happy. Maybe they were going to tell Jessica that she was adopted. But no. All the books said that five was the best age for that, and Mum had read all the books, for sure.

"Don't we have an agenda?" inquired Simon, recalling the days when Dad thought they should all learn parliamentary procedure.

"No," said Dad, "we only have one item of business tonight. The thing is that someone's coming in July."

"Auntie Eileen!" Jessica squealed. Auntie Eileen was the very best relative she had. She liked playing Monopoly and going for walks to the drugstore better than she liked just sitting around and talking to grown-ups. She was a dental hygienist and lived in Toronto. Jessica had been to stay with her twice. It had been great, sleeping on a hide-a-bed and going out to restaurants. Best of all, Auntie Eileen didn't line up any other kids for her to play with.

"No," said Mum, "this visitor is going to stay longer than Auntie Eileen." Through Jessica's head flashed an appalling vision of foster children. Oh, *no*. That would be just like Mum and Dad. Clutter up the house with kids who would be bratty and break your stuff and yet you could never be mad at them because they were underprivileged.

Dad's grin got wider and goofier and one foot traced a circle in the air. Mum sat as usual, straight back, legs crossed at the angle. But even she had a different, secret smile.

Simon stared at his watch and gave a very public sigh.

A FAMILY PROJECT

Up from the basement came the familiar twang of Charlene's guitar:
"You walked into my life,
When you hit my front end.
Now my fender is fixed,
But my heart it won't mend.
We've had a front-end collision (gulp)
Front-end collision (gulp)
Front-end collision
Of love."

Dad grinned. "Oh, let's just get on with it. Thing is, well . . ."

Mum's firm voice broke in. "I'm pregnant."

For a second "pregnant" sounded like a nonsense word to Jessica—"T'was pregnant and the slithy toves . . ." Then it hit her. A baby! She blurted out the first thing that came into her head. "But how can you have a baby? I mean, you've got gray hair."

"Oh, Jessica." Mum gave a half-laugh and then stopped, looking like someone who had forgotten her lines.

Dad jumped in, "To tell you the truth, it kind of took us by surprise, too. But the best-laid plans and all that. Just hope I haven't forgotten my diapering technique."

By this time Mum had recovered. "Forty-one *is* older than usual and the risks are greater, but STATISTICALLY . . ."

All of a sudden Jessica was filled to the fingertips with happiness. She felt like a little kid. There had been a time when she was younger, six and seven, when she had asked for a baby sister, but Mum and Dad had said, "Three's just fine," so she had more or less given up wanting it. But that desire for a baby to hold heavy in her lap swept over her again. She felt a tickling in her throat like the beginning of crying.

Meanwhile Rowan and Simon were saying all the right things. "That's great." "Congratulations." Rowan started to get silly, as he always did when serious stuff was being discussed. "What about names? Let's see. I got the sixties hippy-dippy name, Simon got the English schoolboy phase, and Jessica got Granny's name when we were rediscovering our roots. If this is to be a child of the eighties, how about some sort of financial name, like Dow Jones, or Debenture."

Simon just sat and smiled. "Hope this kid's going to have some athletic potential. I had hopes for Jessica, but she's just as uncoordinated as the rest of this hopeless family."

"It's going to be a long six months," said Dad.

Jessica couldn't say anything. She started thinking about babies on TV. She thought of Mum standing above a white crib with a baby holding up its arms to her. The baby was lying on a checked ruffled cover in a room full of sunlight and toys. Mum picked up a pile of snowy diapers and said something about fabric softener. The baby gooed. But something about the picture wasn't working. Where was this room, anyway? Mum and Dad's room? Simon's room? Her room? And how come Mum wasn't at the office?

"Hey, who's going to take care of this baby?" Jessica interrupted.

"Well," said Dad, "this is our plan. Mum is having six months' maternity leave, starting sometime in June. In the meantime, I'm going to drive a taxi to make some money to put away. Then when Mum goes back to the office, I'm going to stop driving completely and stay home and take care of the baby and anyone else who needs taking care of."

"Where will the baby sleep?"

"In Lavinia's room to start with. It's not safe for me to use the computer anyway while I'm pregnant, so we'll have a chance to get it ready," Mum answered. "Then we'll work out something else later."

Jessica saw Mum looking at her with a worried expression, and she suddenly knew that she had more of a chance to be a brat than she had ever had before. She could pretend to be upset. Below her happiness there *was* something a little sad and scared. She was used to their family the way it was. She liked being the youngest. If she was another middle kid, would she have to be like Simon? The slightly sickening thought hit her that she could pretend to be an upset person pretending to be happy, that she could keep the real happiness way down inside and not let it show. And everyone would be worried and she would have a *problem*, just like in all the books. Articles on "sibling rivalry" would start appearing in the bathroom.

But then she looked around the living room, at Rowan

sprawled on the couch, at Simon, his real face showing for once, doing deep knee-bends behind a chair, at Dad pushing his glasses up his nose, and at Mum with that pleading look. Suddenly she didn't have the heart for it. She jumped up and ran over to Mum, put her head close to Mum's stomach and yelled, "Halloooooo, Baby!" Then Mum grabbed her in a tight hug and Dad went to make special cocoa with whipped cream and chocolate shavings.

3

*J*essica woke up early the next morning to two warm feelings and one worry. The first warm feeling was because it was Saturday. The second was the thought of the baby, and the worry was, "Oh, no, I forgot to phone Margaret."

"Platypus research center, Margaret speaking," Jessica wondered what would happen if somebody else called Margaret's house first thing on Saturday morning. Mum always made them answer the phone properly. "Robertson residence," although Jessica had noticed that Simon answered it, "yeah" if he thought nobody would notice.

"Big news, Margaret, come over right away."

"Check." Margaret didn't waste words when things were serious.

Jessica pulled on her jeans and a T-shirt, mumbled good morning to Dad who was hidden behind the morning paper, grabbed a banana and went out to the front steps to wait for Margaret. Ollie came to sit in her lap. The street was still asleep. The only sounds were from the sky, a seaplane roaring across the clouds and two angry-sounding crows. Ollie stopped kneading Jessica's stomach and settled down. Jessica scratched his hard forehead.

From the far end of the street Jessica saw Margaret's bike, a big old black English bike with a wicker carrier. It stood out from all the BMX's and mountain bikes in the school rack like a heron standing among pigeons. Of course, so did Margaret. Jessica remembered the first time she had seen her. It was Halloween in the fourth grade. After lunch Mr. Sugimoto, the principal ("You can remember how to spell 'principal' because I'm your pal!"), brought in the new girl. "Class, this is a new student, Margaret Lee. Margaret comes to us from Dawson Creek and I know you'll all make her feel very welcome."

Well, the class didn't. For one thing, Margaret didn't look friendly. New kids usually looked shy and sort of like they would be grateful if you talked to them. But Margaret just said, "Thank you, Mr. Sugimoto," in a confident way, looked around the class as though she couldn't care less what they thought, sat down in the new kid's desk, opened her notebook, and looked up at Miss Gilpin.

No one paid much attention to her at all after that, because on the afternoon of Halloween you had too many plans to think about. After trying to make the class interested in spelling for a while, finally even Miss Gilpin gave up and said, "Oh, why don't you just tell me about your costumes."

There weren't many surprises. Eddie Ramponi was going as Frankenstein's monster, with plastic bolts glued to the side of his neck. Cherry Dorkley was going as a princess. Her mother was actually sewing her a costume, with sequins and everything. Jessica was wearing Simon's hand-me-down glow-in-the-dark skeleton costume, and almost everyone else was being either witches or punks.

"How about you, Margaret?" asked Miss Gilpin. "What are you going to be on your first Vancouver Halloween?"

"I'm going to be a pencil."

"A pencil. Well, that's certainly a different idea." Miss Gilpin laughed a bit nervously and looked at Margaret as though she expected something more. Margaret looked steadily back at Miss Gilpin and didn't say anything. Margaret looked kind of proud, sitting very tall in her desk. Right at that moment Jessica knew she wanted her for a friend.

After school Jessica saw Margaret striding up the road and ran to catch up with her. "Hey, are you really going to be a pencil tonight?"

"No, of course not. We just moved this weekend and nothing is unpacked. I just said pencil because it was the first thing that came into my head. It's a good idea to try to surprise teachers, don't you think? Otherwise they get bored."

About a block from Jessica's house, they both hit on

the idea that maybe Margaret could be a pencil after all. "Come on over to my place," said Jessica. "We've got lots of stuff."

In Jessica's yellow jumpsuit and pink socks and a black paper cone on her head, Margaret made a very good pencil. She ended up staying for dinner and Dad called her Maggie Muggins and it seemed as though she had always been there.

That night as they trick-or-treated around the neighborhood, Jessica discovered that Margaret was very good at talking about plans and projects. She was also good at discussing important things, like whether it would be better to burn to death or to freeze to death. But she didn't like to talk about things like family. That first day Jessica asked about Margaret's father, but Margaret just said "Gone," and it was clear she didn't want any more questions.

Sometimes even after more than a year, Jessica still felt shy with Margaret. As she saw her riding show-off nohands down the middle of the street, she suddenly felt shy again. What would Margaret say? Would she think it was dumb to have a new baby in the family? Would she be jealous?

Margaret skidded into the driveway and dropped her bike. "So, what's the news?"

Jessica noticed that Margaret was wearing mismatched socks, a green neon ankle sock with lace around the top and a thick argyle knee sock. Jessica didn't know what to say before she said, "My mum's going to have a baby," so she just blurted it out, not looking at Margaret.

"A baby! Hey, that's totally . . ." But Jessica never found out what having a baby was totally, because in trying to jump over her bike in excitement, Margaret got caught up in one of the pedals and ended up completely tangled with her bike in the middle of the driveway. The leg with the ankle sock on it took it the hardest.

Inside, Dad emerged from behind the paper to find Mercurochrome and Band-Aids. Margaret gave several karate whoops as Dad cleaned the gravel out of her knee, but she didn't cry. Dad used Band-Aids with bears printed on them. Margaret had never seen them before and she was impressed.

All through the attention to Margaret's knee, Jessica kept hoping that she would talk about the baby. It didn't seem fair that once Jessica had brought up a shy subject, she should have to do it again. She began to feel left out as Dad joked with Margaret. She almost wished that Margaret had just stayed home.

So she didn't say anything as they wheeled their bikes onto the street. They rode in their usual way toward the library and the park. But then Margaret zoomed ahead in a different direction.

"Hey, Margaret, where are you going?"

"Just follow me."

Margaret was heading up toward the mall. That wasn't like her. Margaret didn't like the mall any more than

Jessica did. Full of rough kids in the video arcade and un-friendly shop clerks who thought you were stealing just because you were a kid. They always came up and said, "May I help you?" in a nasty way that meant, "Why don't you leave?"

Jessica had never realized this bothered any other kids until Margaret did an oral presentation in class on "kid-ism." Mr. Blackburn had asked them to write about something in their lives that they thought was unfair. Almost everyone had written boring things about too much home-work or not having enough allowance or being youngest/middle/oldest in their families. But Margaret had spoken about the way kids are treated in shops and movies and on the bus.

"It's kidism," she declared, "and kidism is prejudice just like racism or sexism."

Mr. Blackburn said the speech showed "great maturity and conviction," but of course Margaret blew it the next week by arguing that having to spell correctly was inter-fering with her creativity.

Jessica and Margaret avoided kidists as much as they could by mostly hanging out at the library and in the park where their grown-up friends were Anne the librarian, who let them play with leftover graphics supplies and Willie the bird man in the park, who put seeds on his hat and let the birds land all over him.

Jessica was therefore surprised to see Margaret chaining her bike up outside the mall. And even more surprised to follow her as she marched by the record store and the sticker store without a glance. She began to understand, though, when Margaret parked herself in front of Kiddie Kloset. As Jessica looked in the window at the stuffed toys and rainbow bibs and, best of all, miniature running shoes, the mad feeling at Margaret dissolved.

"Come on," said Margaret, "we have to do some research."

"Excuse me," she said to the shop clerk. "Could you show us the things for babies that are just born?" The saleswoman was not a kidist. She didn't smile at them as though she thought they were cute, but just as though she was happy.

As they looked at nighties and booties and sleepers, Margaret managed to tell the clerk all about Jessica's baby. And even though they didn't buy anything, the clerk didn't get impatient. In the library, where they went next, Margaret got Anne looking up all the books on babies and the whole story was told again. Talking about a baby made a lot of people happy, Jessica noticed.

Anne gave them books of nursery rhymes and then took them to the adult department. By the time they had finished, they had *Never Too Young: Read to Your Baby, Babies and Music, The Art of Baby Massage, Non-Sexist Child Rearing, Life Before Birth: Essays on Birth Memory* and a book on decorating nurseries. Their bike baskets were so full that their bikes nearly fell over whenever they turned a corner.

At Jessica's house they spread out the books all over her bed. "Forget the duck-billed platypus," said Margaret. "We're going to do our project on babies."

"But babies aren't animals."

"Yes, they are. If humans are animals, then babies are animals."

"Oh yeah, *that*." "That" for Jessica meant all those bits of trick information. Tomatoes are fruit. Spiders are not insects. People are animals. These were the kind of facts that Cherry Dorkley specialized in. Whereas any normal person knows that you don't put tomatoes in a fruit salad and that spiders live in the garage with the black beetles and are therefore insects.

"I don't think that's what Mr. Blackburn meant."

"Of course he didn't. But he'll love it. He'll think it's really cute. He probably doesn't want to read thirty-four projects on animals, anyway. I mean, how interested can someone *be* in the life cycle of the salmon for the zillionth time? Anyway, he'll like it because we can relate it to our own lives. We will be making our education . . ."

"RELEVANT!" they both chorused.

"Okay," said Jessica, "but you'll have to do the talking."

"No sweat."

4

A few weeks later, Jessica began to wish they had stuck to the duck-billed platypus. The baby project was getting out of hand. Mr. Blackburn loved the idea so much that he let them have time off from other subjects and gave them an extra month for the project.

"It's creative, it's relevant, it's interdisciplinary," he enthused. "It covers science, history, social studies."

"Spelling," Margaret whispered, but Mr. Blackburn was on a roll and didn't hear her.

To begin, Jessica and Margaret used their regular technique of dividing the project into parts. Jessica decided to take appearance, food, habits and habitat. Margaret would cover enemies, natural defenses, life cycle and topics of special interest.

▲ FRANK SMITH, JR. LIBRARY CENTER
SOUTHWESTERN UNIVERSITY
GEORGETOWN, TEXAS 78626

3 3053 00238 3222

In the past, the problem with projects was usually that you couldn't find enough information. One of the great things about Margaret as a partner was that she had big handwriting. But the baby project just kept growing.

Jessica started the "Appearance" section by looking at a book that had big colored pictures of what the baby looked like when it was waiting to be born. At first the pictures made Jessica feel a bit sick. They looked too much like a baby to be anything else, but not enough like a baby to be right. There was too much about them that was like a frog. But she couldn't stop looking at them and trying to make sense of what was happening to Mum. She showed them to Simon, but he just said they were gross.

And then there was heredity. Heredity was things like, "He's got Uncle Wally's nose," or "Simon, you're as stubborn as your mother." Heredity was also kind of like math, and Jessica particularly liked the Mendel Box. She phoned Margaret to describe it.

"Okay, let's take eye color. If you have one blue-eyed parent and one brown-eyed parent, chances are you'll have three brown-eyed children and one blue-eyed. Brown wins because it is 'dominant.' Isn't that neat? And it works in our family, too. Dad has green eyes and that counts as blue."

"Sounds like cheating."

"I know, but that's how it works. Mum had brown. That means that we should have three browns and a blue. Rowan's got brown. Simon's got blue. I've got hazel. That counts as brown."

"Sounds like cheating again."

"*Margaret*. Just listen for a minute. That means the baby will probably have brown eyes."

"Okay," said Margaret. "Let's try it for fat and skinny."

"But you have to know what is dominant."

"Well, fat, obviously. Look how grown-ups talk about fat all the time and dieting and exercise. It's like *everybody* would be fat if they didn't fight it."

"Okay, let's try my family again. I guess I count as skinny . . ."

Simon's voice cut in. "You sure do: 22, 22, 22. A figure to drive men wild."

"Simon! Get off this phone. DAD! Simon's listening in."

"Yeah, well, you've had your fifteen minutes anyway." This time Simon's voice reached Jessica in stereo, through the phone into one ear and booming up from downstairs into the other.

"So? You talk to Patrick for hours."

Dad came to referee but Jessica and Margaret decided to continue their discussion in person. But when they got together, Margaret declared that heredity was boring and that she was much more interested in environment.

"Environment starts even before the baby is born, Jess. We've got to get busy."

Jessica would have been content to recite educational things like multiplication tables at Mum's stomach from time to time. But Margaret took a more organized approach.

She decided the baby needed great books, so they started with the encyclopedia. They began with volume one and read the baby about Aachen, the West German city; Alvar Aalto, the Finnish architect; and the aardvark.

Trouble was, Mum started to get bored. "It's hard for me to do anything else while my stomach is being read to." Jessica immediately felt silly. Did Mum think the baby project was dumb? Was she just putting up with them? But Margaret didn't feel silly. She looked for a solution.

"Why don't you knit?" she asked. "That's what pregnant women are supposed to do."

"I don't knit," said Mum shortly.

"Don't, or can't?" asked Margaret.

Jessica felt her stomach tighten. Maybe Margaret could talk like that to her own mother, but not in the Robertson family. But Mum replied with a smile. "Well, *can't*, actually. I tried once when I was expecting Rowan but the stitches just kept getting tighter and tighter until I couldn't slide them off the needles. I still feel anxious when I see those knitting patterns—'yn fwd, k 2 tog.' They're like some secret torture code."

"Hey, that's right," said Margaret. "Did you know that in the war those secret army guys got hold of a knitting pattern from Germany and thought it was a secret code?"

"I hope the baby is finding this educational," said Jessica, being a bit jokey but mostly mad. Mum never told *her* about trying to knit. Mum never told her that she was anxious or not good at something. Mum probably just told smart kids like Margaret that kind of stuff. How did Margaret know about that war business, anyway?

Mum gave her a mind-reading look. "Good point, Jessica. We've got a long way to go in this encyclopedia. What's after aardvark?"

"Aardwolf," said Jessica.

Mum sighed. "Carry on."

Stimulating the baby musically was a bit easier on Mum. At first Jessica and Margaret tried to persuade her to take up the cello, because they had read about a famous conductor whose mother had played the cello when she was pregnant with him. But Mum said you couldn't learn to play the cello in three months.

So instead they decided to play records for the baby. Anne the librarian really got into the baby project herself and suggested tapes of lullabies and Raffi songs from the children's room. But Margaret got an idea that the music should be grown-up, so they went up to the record library and asked for the most serious music there was. The record librarian sent them home with a symphony by some dead composer named Mahler. Mum liked it better than subjects beginning with "A," but Jessica and Margaret hated it. It was loud, boring, and long. "We'll leave the music part to you," they said.

When Jessica looked back later on the mess that the baby project caused, she realized that as long as she and

Margaret had stuck to books and records, it had been okay. She could hold out against some of Margaret's stranger ideas. For example, she did have to put her foot down when Margaret brought up the topic of mating habits. "*Margaret.* Forget it. That's, you know, sex. Anyway, it's not even on our list of topics."

"Of course it's not listed. You think Mr. Blackburn is going to let Eddie talk about sex in a school report?"

"Don't see why not. He talks about it everywhere else."

"Yeah. But we're different. We could deal with the topic in a mature way."

"We could not. Besides, this is my parents we're talking about. No way."

"Well then, listen. There's a chapter here about how people under hypnosis can remember their own birth. Let's try it."

As Jessica realized later, that was when the real trouble began. Field studies turned out to be dangerous.

They pulled the blinds in Jessica's room and Margaret swung her watch in front of her eyes. "You're feeling very tired and relaxed. Your head is heavy. Your hands are heavy. You are a tiny baby being born. You want to get out."

But it didn't work. "Jessica, you are *resisting.*"

"I'm *not* resisting. There's just nothing relaxing about your watch flapping back and forth in front of my face."

"Okay, we need something on a chain."

The only thing they could think of was the bathtub

plug, so Jessica got the pliers and removed it. But somehow watching a bathtub plug swinging back and forth in front of your eyes doesn't make you very relaxed, either. It makes you giggly. It also gets you into trouble the next morning when you have forgotten to return the plug to the tub and Dad wants a bath.

"I had the most unusual bath this morning. I had to keep my heel over the drain. I don't suppose anyone knows the whereabouts of the plug?"

Margaret didn't give up. "You're too old, that's the trouble. Your birth was too long ago. We need some little kids."

So one day, Margaret took her clipboard to school. ("All reporters have clipboards.") She tried to interview the kindergarten kids on the playground at lunch.

"Do you remember being born?" When they looked confused by the question, Margaret went into greater detail. But it turned out the greater detail made some of the kindergarten kids cry. They told their parents. The parents told the principal. And Mr. Sugimoto turned out not to be a pal after all and complained to Mr. Blackburn. Mr. Blackburn stood up for them as much as he could, but they still had to write five letters of apology to kindergarten parents.

"Ridiculous," fumed Margaret. "If they don't know where babies come from by the time they are five years old they certainly *should*. They should *thank* us. These kids would probably grow up with *complexes* if it wasn't for us."

Jessica let Margaret rant. With Margaret, there were times when it was best to say nothing. But as she sat writing, "Dear Mrs. Vienne, I'm sorry we made Tiffany cry," she half-wished the baby project was over. At school more than half the class had presented their reports. Eddie's was a masterpiece. He spent about ten seconds on the habitat, life cycle and size of the shark, and about eight gory minutes on examples of shark attacks on humans.

"And my uncle knew this guy who had to have 881 stitches after a shark bit him across the chest and shoulders."

Mr. Blackburn looked as though teacher-training school hadn't told him what to do about kids like Eddie. "That was, er, very colorful, Eddie."

But the biggest trouble with the baby project was still to come. It all started with the "enemies" section.

"I don't think that section applies, Margaret. Mr. Blackburn said we didn't have to do every topic, right? It's not like eagles drop out of the sky and pluck babies from their strollers, you know."

Margaret started chewing the ends of her hair. Jessica always got nervous when Margaret chewed her hair. It usually ended in trouble.

"Look, Jess, I've been thinking about the mall."

"What about it?"

"Well, you know how kidist they are?"

"Yup."

"That's not the worst thing. They are also babyist."

"Come on, Margaret, they don't try to kick babies out of the mall."

"No, they do worse. What do you see in the mall? Mothers sitting on uncomfortable seats looking mad and feeding their babies orange swoozle and hot dogs."

Jessica didn't mention that this was a favorite lunch of Margaret herself.

Margaret continued, "Why don't they sell baby food in the Food Fair?"

Jessica thought of mushed-up peas. "Yuck."

"Just my point. That's babyism. Out and out babyism. Just because it doesn't look good to you, you want to deny babies good nutrition. And another thing— where are mothers supposed to change their babies in the mall?"

"Oh, come on, Margaret, we're not going to get into diapers, are we?"

"It's all part of a baby's life, Jess."

"Are you going to write about that stuff in the report?" Jessica asked nervously.

"No, we are going to try to change it. This situation is disgraceful. We should make a fuss, get some publicity. We should make that mall put in diaper changing tables and a baby food restaurant."

Jessica wasn't enthusiastic, but Margaret had a way of getting you to do things even if you didn't want to.

"Margaret, I think we have enough for our project already."

"Come on, Jess. Don't you want a better mall for babies?"

"Okay, but you'll have to do all the talking."

"Sure, sure. You can be the technician."

Jessica's first job as technician was to persuade Simon to lend them his portable tape recorder. It was a hard bargain. First Jessica offered to do his dishwashing duty for three extra days. But Simon still wouldn't agree until she told him about their plans for the mall.

When she got to a description of kidism, Simon grinned. "You think you've got it bad. Try being a teenager. Then they really hate you. What would you call that? Young adultism? What kind of questions are you going to ask, anyway?"

Jessica pulled out Margaret's list. "Why don't you drop by and watch?"

Simon's face closed in. "No way. I've got things to do on Saturday."

Margaret practiced her interview on Jessica. "This is Margaret Lee, live from the Leisureland Mall. I'm speaking this morning to Mr. Reg McLean, the manager of the mall. Good morning, Mr. McLean. How are you?"

Jessica put on her deep voice. "I'm just fine, Ms. Lee. How are you?"

"Let's get right down to it, Mr. McLean. Do you think it's being a responsible corporate citizen to run a mall where there's no place to change a baby, where there's no food that is good for a baby, where there's no place to nurse a baby? I suggest, Mr. McLean, that this is babyism, babyism at its worst."

"Margaret, don't you think that's being a bit rude?"

"Jess, don't you listen to interviews on TV? When grown-ups talk like that it's not rude. It's hard-hitting."

"But are you really going to talk about breast-feeding? I mean, isn't that kind of embarrassing?"

"Reporters are above all that, Jess. We just go out there for the stories."

As it turned out, Margaret didn't get a chance to be hard-hitting. The manager of the mall wouldn't talk to them. Jessica was relieved, but not for long.

"I'll fix him," said Margaret. "I'll say that the manager refused comment. We'll go to the source."

On Saturday morning, Margaret and Jessica biked up to the mall. Margaret had her clipboard and Simon's tape recorder in her basket. First of all they went into the supermarket. They saw a young woman with a baby in a backpack choosing lettuce. Jessica turned on the tape recorder.

"Excuse me," said Margaret. "We're doing a study of how the mall treats babies. Do you have any complaints?"

The woman gave them a friendly smile. "Not really. What do you mean?"

"Well, like, wouldn't it be a good idea if these grocery carts had seat belts for small children?"

"Sure. I guess so."

"Thank *you*," said Margaret triumphantly. She and Jessica walked off. Margaret spoke into the tape recorder.

"One hundred percent of those interviewed thought that grocery cart safety could be improved."

There were no other babies in the store, so Jessica and Margaret bought granola bars. Margaret spoke to the checker about seat belts.

"Yeah, great idea. Keep them tied down as far as I'm concerned. Anything to keep the monsters from messing up my check-out."

After they paid, Margaret spoke into the tape recorder again. "Store employees agree."

It wasn't as bad as Jessica had expected. When they visited Kiddie Kloset, the clerk was so nice that Margaret forgot about being hard-hitting. The clerk agreed it was a shame that there weren't comfortable places in the mall for babies and she gave Margaret a few statistics on how much of their business was in baby clothes. Then they had a long conversation about whether girls should wear pink and boys blue. Jessica didn't think this had anything to do with the topic, but Margaret said it was human interest, to flesh out the interview.

"But now for the serious stuff," said Margaret. Jessica's heart sank.

First of all they went to the women's washroom. They waited outside until they saw a woman with a baby in a stroller go in. They rushed in after her.

"Just wait," said Margaret. "She's going to have to change the baby on the floor."

But the woman just washed her hands and started to

leave. Margaret couldn't stand it. "Hey, doesn't your baby need changing?"

The woman turned around in a rage. "He certainly does not. What business is it of yours, anyway?"

"No, I just meant that if he *did* need changing . . ." But the woman had flounced away.

"Margaret, can we stop now?"

"No, Jess. We're just getting started. Don't get upset. Reporters get yelled at all the time. Let's just go to the Food Fair."

Jessica really wanted to go home, but Margaret was determined to get an interview. She approached a woman with a baby and two toddlers. They were sitting at a table eating hot dogs and drinking milk shakes.

"Good morning," said Margaret. "We're doing a survey on the quality of food in the mall as it applies to babies. Do you have any opinions on that?"

The woman grabbed a milk shake just as it was overturning. She had a large pile of paper napkins in front of her. "What?"

"Don't you think it's bad that there is no baby food in the mall?"

The middle toddler grabbed the rescued milk shake and began making burbling noises with the straw. "Suck, Jason, don't blow." Jason continued blowing bubbles. "Jason, if you keep doing that I'm taking that drink away from you." The woman wrestled the drink from Jason, who began to wail. She slathered mustard on a piece of bun to quiet him. She looked up. "What was it you wanted?"

Jessica tugged on Margaret's jacket. "Come *on*. She's too busy," she whispered. Margaret held her ground. "Don't you think that the mall should sell better food for children?"

The woman thought for a moment as the older toddler began to kick the underside of the table. The salt and mustard and ketchup packages began to dance on the tabletop. "It's okay. They like it. It's cheap."

Margaret opened her mouth but Jessica grabbed her and pulled her away. Next they went to stand by the mall entrance. Most people wouldn't talk to them, but they did have a few conversations with mothers and one dad. The morning wore on and Jessica went back to the Food Fair for ice cream cones to give them strength. When she got back to the entrance, Margaret was talking to a fat man in a suit. Margaret looked excited.

". . . so you think this mall is mean to babies, do you?" the man was saying.

"Yes, it certainly is. The situation is terrible. The people who manage this mall should be ashamed." Margaret was warming up. Jessica looked at the man and realized that something was terribly wrong.

"And how long have you been standing here talking to people?"

"Oh, all morning."

"And who gave you permission to do this?"

Margaret faded. "Well, nobody."

"All right, young lady, you just come with me. I am the manager of this mall and we are going to phone your parents. I've had it with trouble-making kids." He reached out for Margaret's arm.

Margaret gave Jessica one desperate look and Jessica yelled the first thing that came into her head. "Run!"

Margaret shook off the man's arm and the girls raced down the mall toward the opposite exit. Their sandals slapped on the tiles and Jessica lost one of the ice cream cones.

"Security!" roared the manager and there, at the other exit, was a man in a uniform.

For one wild moment Jessica thought of ducking into the supermarket to hide, but Margaret just stopped dead in her tracks. "They've got us."

In the manager's office, Jessica cried and babbled out her phone number. Margaret sat sullen-faced and refused to say anything.

"Your mother is coming," the manager said to Jessica.

My mum? thought Jessica in surprise. She still wasn't used to Mum being the one who was home. Would she be really mad?

When Mum arrived she was wearing the most pregnant of her pregnant dresses and the manager looked a little taken aback at her large size. She sat very quietly and listened to everything the manager said. ". . . these damn kids always making trouble, blah, blah . . . no permission

. . . blah, blah . . . we are a business, not a community center. . . ."

Mum let the manager run down and then she left a long pause in which the manager made little noises in the back of his throat.

Then Mum began to speak. She used a lot of capitals. "I can understand why you are UPSET over this and the girls certainly made an ERROR in JUDGMENT. But I have no intention of punishing them. The points they make about the management of this mall are absolutely VALID and I would advise you to consider them SERIOUSLY in your role as corporate citizen. Come, girls." Mum stood up and swept out of the office.

As they left they heard the manager sputtering, "I don't ever want to see those girls in my mall again."

Jessica said, "Don't want to come here anyway," in a low voice and felt better.

In the parking lot, Mum had other things to say about how worried she had been when the manager phoned and about how they should tell her when they had projects like this. But Jessica hardly listened. She kept remembering how Mum had looked when she stood up to leave the office, just like a queen.

When Jessica returned Simon's recorder, he insisted on listening to the tape. She expected him to laugh at their disaster, but instead he seemed to really enjoy the interviews.

A FAMILY PROJECT

"Hey, listen to the way that mall guy calls Margaret 'young lady.' What a jerk."

Later he dropped by Jessica's room and threw a couple of sheets of press-on letters onto her desk. "Maybe you can use this for the project. I was going to throw it away. It's a bit wrecked."

Jessica was surprised, but she was careful not to make too much of it. "Okay, thanks."

When the project was finally finished, Jessica and Margaret left out the bit about babyism in the mall. But even without it, the project looked great. The title page, done in press-on letters, said, "The Baby Project, by Jessica Ruth Robertson and Margaret Jean Lee." Glued all over the page were tiny photos of babies cut out of magazines.

It was eighteen pages long, the longest thing either of them had ever done. It had transcripts of the tape with the Kiddie Kloset clerk, diagrams of the developing baby, a chart of height and weight (that was math), photocopies of the article on remembering your own birth, and a note saying that this was inconclusive. And it had a clear plastic cover on the outside.

When Jessica read it over she was so proud she couldn't believe they had done it. She wondered if it was too show-offy to feel so proud of something she had made. But as it turned out, Mr. Blackburn liked it too, and showed it to the principal, who invited them to his office and shook their hands and told them about the value of initiative.

They decided to keep the project at Jessica's house because Margaret didn't have room. And then when Margaret had her own house, which was going to be huge, and on an island, with lots of sheep and dogs, she could have the project any time she wanted it.

"We'll time-share it," said Margaret.

5

*W*aiting. Jessica sat at her desk and made the word "waiting" with her printing set. She popped the little rubber letters into their holder. "gnitiaw." Waiting for the beginning of summer holidays was bad enough, but waiting for a baby to be born was worse.

Jessica whacked the red ink pad and stamped "waiting" on her blotter. It was not only worse than waiting for summer holidays, it was worse than waiting for your birthday. It was even worse than waiting for Christmas. At least with Christmas you could open little doors on the Advent calendar and no matter what else happened, by the time that last door was open, Christmas had come. But babies! You didn't even know when, for sure. Mum said July 3, maybe.

Waiting. Jessica took down her "Mammals of British Columbia" calendar. The June beaver looked busy. She began stamping the days. June 6—Waiting. June 7—Waiting. June 8—Waiting . . . The July elk looked bored. July 1—Waiting. July 2—Waiting.

June 6th to July 3rd. Twenty-eight days left to wait. Twenty-eight times twenty-four hours times sixty minutes times sixty seconds. Thank goodness for sleep.

Jessica re-inked the stamp and stamped her arm across the untanned line where her watch usually was. By the time. By the time the orthodontist put braces on Simon's teeth, the baby would be born. By the time Dad's sweet peas grew to the top of the trellis, the baby would be born.

By the time her library book was due, the baby would be born. Maybe. Jessica looked down at her hand. By the time the little white spots on her thumbnail had grown out, she calculated, the baby would be here. Two spots, not good. "One for love, two for danger, three for the moneybags, four kiss a stranger."

The telephone rang. Jessica got her foot caught under her desk and Simon reached it first.

"Jessie!" he bellowed.

It was Margaret. "What are you doing?"

"Waiting."

"For what?"

"The baby."

"I'll come over and help you."

Jessica and Margaret got themselves organized in the

back yard with blankets and books and a radio and lemonade (the frozen kind—the food scene was a little more
normal with Mum in charge). Charlene came out the
basement door. "I'm going to a dream interpretation work-
shop. I think as a songwriter I need to be more in touch
with the inner me. Oh, by the way, I've got something for
you." She dug around in her purse and came up with a
bottle of black nail polish. "It didn't sell that well. See
you."

The girls spent some time on their fingernails. Jessica
covered up her dangerous spotted thumb. Then they lay
with their legs in the sun for tanning and their heads in the
shade for reading.

Jessica lay on her front for chapter one, her back for
chapter two, and then wondered if the book was a mistake.
The trouble with animal survival stories was that animals
didn't talk much.

"What we really need is a waiter," said Margaret.

"A waiter?" said Jessica, thinking of someone rushing
around with plates and filling up your water glass.

"Yeah, someone who waits. You pay them to wait until
July 3rd for you and then you can be at July 3rd right
away."

"But then they get left behind in time, don't they? I
mean, here we would be at July 3rd with the baby born
and all, maybe, and the poor waiter would still be back on
June 6th."

Margaret blew on her nails, "No, when July 3rd came

for them they could jump ahead to where everyone else was. Like we'd already be in August and they could jump over to August, too. It would be like playing 'Mother, May I.' Mostly you go along with baby steps, but sometimes you get to take a giant step."

Jessica thought for a minute. "Sounds like the kind of job that would give you a stomachache."

Margaret wasn't listening. "No, that's not right. They wouldn't just leap ahead automatically. They would take on anti-waiting jobs. They would get those jobs with people who didn't *want* time to pass so quickly. Like if on July 3rd you were having a perfect day but you knew that the next week something bad was going to happen like . . . someone was going to move away, you could just pay the waiter to move ahead to the next week for you, and then you could just stay in the happy week until you were ready."

Something in Margaret's voice had changed. She wasn't just goofing around any more. Was she trying to tell Jessica about her father?

"Has that ever happened to you? Just wanting time to stop?"

Margaret answered without a pause. "Sure. The day before school pictures." She gave a little laugh.

Jessica saw two roads ahead of her. A sunny road full of talk about the creepiness of the school photographer, about Cherry Dorkley getting her hair permed for the occasion, about possible monster faces Margaret could make. And a darker road where Margaret could tell her, really, about why her voice went sad.

But Margaret was continuing on about waiters. "It might be hard to find waiters because they would have all the boring and sad bits to live through. But there would be one excellent thing about the job."

"What?"

"You would never have to die. When you got old or sick you could just take on waiting jobs, never anti-waiting jobs."

Jessica felt as though she was playing chess with Simon (when Simon would still play chess with her). She was trying to hold hard ideas in her head. If the knight moves there, then this might happen, but if I move the rook there, then this might happen, and it would prevent this from happening. If you lived in the waiting time then you never had to die, but if you lived in the anti-waiting time, the sad time, then death came closer?

Suddenly Jessica got goose bumps, even on the sun-hot parts of her. It was too hard and it was too scary. She let the idea drain out of her mind like water. "Hey, Margaret, let's do our toenails, too."

By the end of June everyone started to get grumpy, and Dad began to make bleak little jokes about elephants being pregnant for eighteen months.

The name discussion seemed endless. "It was bad enough when two people had to agree," said Dad. "Now we've got five voting members." Mum tried to make everyone be serious. "We've got to think not just about naming a baby, but naming a grown adult as well. It's fine to think of a baby named Pookie," Mum stared at Rowan, who had suggested this for a girl, "but it's an odd name for a middle-aged woman. And you should say the name aloud to see how it sounds with Robertson. What we really need is a list."

And so a list was taped to the fridge, but it quickly filled up with silliness. Auntie Eileen participated by mail, sending postcards saying, "How about Hortense?" or "Why not Montmorency?" Finally Dad confessed that he really wanted "Lucie" for a girl. Simon rolled his eyes. "You mean like 'I Love Lucy'?"

"No, Simon, like in Wordsworth," Dad continued, while Simon pretended to throw up. "Anyway 'ie,' not 'y.' Lucie: it means 'light.'"

No decision could be reached on a boy's name. "I've used up all my favorites," complained Mum. So mostly they just called the baby the "no-name baby."

At first Jessica stayed home all the time, in case she missed something. But after a while she got fed up. Mum had her bag all packed, but then the family ran out of toothpaste and used hers and then Mum wanted to read the book she had been saving for the hospital and one day the bag disappeared from the hall and didn't make its way back there.

. . .

When it finally happened, it was as though the baby was born in a time that was not in real time. First there was July sixth, a whole ordinary day with meals and flossing your teeth and fights with Simon. Then there was July seventh, a day of chaos. But the night in between got stretched, like pulling gum out of your mouth in a long strand.

Dad woke Jessica. "Wake up, Jess-Mess. We're going to the hospital soon. Come say goodbye to Mum."

Downstairs everything seemed very ordinary, except that it was the middle of the night. Mum was sitting on the couch drinking a cup of tea. Jessica had expected people to be running around the house panicking and dropping things like on TV. She thought Mum would be moaning and doubled over. Instead she sat very calm and motioned Jessica to come sit beside her.

Suddenly a funny look traveled over Mum's face. "That's it."

"It, what's it?"

"Shhhh," replied Simon who was sitting with his track-timing stopwatch. He wrote down something on a piece of paper. "Five minutes that time."

"It means the contractions are five minutes apart," explained Mum.

"Okay," said Dad who seemed to be walking around the room without knowing he was doing it. "Time to hit the road."

"Sit down and I'll just finish my tea," said Mum. Dad did sit down but his foot kept making circles in the air.

55

Jessica heard Rowan's van and the sound of him bounding up the porch steps. He looked pale as he loped in the front door. "Am I in time?"

Mum gave Jessica a hug. "Take care of the boys."

Jessica got a tight throat and couldn't say a word.

By the time they left, Jessica felt wider awake than she had ever felt before. She was disgusted when Simon mumbled something about bed and shuffled off. Rowan was in the kitchen grinding coffee beans. Jessica knelt on the couch and pulled open the curtains. She sank back on her heels and rested her chin on the cool smooth fabric. The streetlight shone through the leaves of the cherry tree in the front yard. In the apartment up the road, two lights were burning. I'm going to remember exactly how this feels for the rest of my life, she vowed.

Rowan made not only coffee but hot almond milk, and he brought them into the living room where they sat for a while in silence. Ollie joined them, looking a bit put out at their invasion of his nighttime house.

"Hey, Row, do you think it really hurts, having a baby?"

"Well, they say it hurts a lot but that mothers don't mind because they like the result."

"Do you think that's true, or do they just tell you that so you won't be scared?"

"I don't know, Jess. Why don't you ask Mum? She's pretty good about telling us the truth."

Jessica sipped her milk. "I think I'll adopt. I don't think I want to go through labor."

56

Rowan held out his hand. "Shake. I don't think I want to either."

Jessica giggled and curled up on the corner of the couch. The last thing she remembered was a blanket being tucked in around her.

The first thing she felt the next day was the house shaking as Dad slammed the front door behind him. "It's a girl. Seven pounds two ounces and nineteen inches long. Baby fine. Mum fine. Dad pooped."

There was a steady round of showers and a breakfast of sorts. Even Dad ate his cereal standing up and drank leftover coffee from the night before. On the way to the hospital again he stopped at the corner store to buy flowers. "Come on, everybody, pick your favorites." They ended up with a huge bunch of every kind of flower that Mr. Iaci sold—red and yellow roses, pepper-smelling freesias, Mum's favorite purple irises, and two fierce-looking tiger lilies. When Mr. Iaci found out the occasion, he added a pink camelia plant, "for the baby."

Dad got goofier and goofier on the way to the hospital. The elevator smelled funny and Jessica felt a bit scared. Before they could go into the room, they had to put on green back-to-front hospital gowns. Dad started singing some corny old song about nymphs and shepherds. Simon got his "I wish I could be teleported elsewhere" look.

When they finally got into the room, Dad and the boys seemed to grow twice as big, like in a funhouse mirror.

And the family seemed to multiply into a crowd, cramming the room with people and noise and flowers.

But it all disappeared for Jessica when she saw the baby, lying in a clear plastic crib right beside Mum, wrapped in a blanket and wearing a white cotton cap.

"Look," said Rowan, "a toque. She looks like a lumberjack."

"Of course," said Dad. "She's a little Canadian baby, after all."

Jessica put her hand into the crib and the baby grabbed her finger very tight. She had damp, very black hair and a scrunched-up face.

"Lucie," whispered Jessica. Dad and the boys didn't hear because they were all clearing places for flowers and putting them into the vases the nurse brought.

But Mum noticed and said very quietly, below the hubbub, "Lucie, I think you've got a friend."

6

*L*ucie made more of a change than Jessica could have predicted. For one thing, although she didn't take up much room herself, she certainly had a lot of stuff. Everyone who came to see the baby brought her a gift. Charlene arrived from downstairs with a large, very pink toy dog. Margaret continued her program of early childhood education by making Lucie a mobile of the ten provinces with bake-in-the-oven clay. She had to make it twice because the first time the oven was too hot and the clay melted.

"Manitoba burnt onto the bottom of the oven."

"Did you get heck?"

"Don't ask."

But Mrs. Lee must not have minded too much, because she sent Lucie a present, too—a lacy crocheted shawl.

The people in Mum's office got together and bought a big English pram. Rowan invented a pack to carry Lucie in. It adjusted in seven ways and had clever pockets with Velcro and zippers. It was black nylon with a big yellow duck appliquéd on the front.

Dad kept finding reasons to drive the taxi to an exclusive baby wear shop downtown. Mum didn't approve. "David, she doesn't really *need* designer undershirts." Only Auntie Eileen's present didn't take any room. She sent stock. "Nothing gives a woman more confidence than her own financial portfolio," she wrote.

The muddle of Lucie's things extended to general muddle in their lives. People seemed to be sleeping at odd times. Dad worked crazy hours and was likely to be sleeping anytime. Mum napped with Lucie in the afternoon and Simon took to watching the late-late movie and sleeping half the day. Jessica got up with the early morning and ate breakfast at seven while Dad, just home from work, was constructing himself a salad. By the time Jessica came in for a noontime sandwich, Simon was sitting bleary-eyed over his cornflakes.

But the biggest difference of all wasn't meals or routines. It was Lucie herself, just being there. She was like a low background hum in Jessica's life. At the pool or downtown shopping with Margaret or reading in bed at night, Lucie was always in Jessica's head, in a way that nobody had ever been before.

And not just in her head. Jessica knew how Lucie felt. Not just like she "knew" when Simon felt hurt or Mum felt impatient, but a deep-down knowing. When she held the baby, when she felt her change from the plastic doll hardness she had when she was crying to the floppy rag doll she became just before she slept, Jessica felt her own self relax.

Sometimes feeling with Lucie was a worry. At first Jessica objected to the way Mum wrapped Lucie up in the blanket, tight and neat like a parcel.

"She'll squish, she'll hate it," Jessica protested.

"No, she likes it," said Mum. "It makes her feel secure." That night Jessica decided to try it. She put her top sheet on the bed diagonally and positioned herself in the middle of it. Then she flipped the bottom over her feet, pulled one side corner across and tucked it under her and then rolled over to complete the wrapping. After several tries and falling out of bed once, she finally made herself into a tidy sausage. She didn't feel much like a baby, more like an Egyptian mummy. Hey—babies and mummies. She fell asleep with the pun dancing in her head.

She awoke later in a panic, climbing out of a quicksand dream and kicking her hot feet wildly to free them. As she lay waiting for her heartbeat to quiet, she heard from downstairs the sound of Lucie crying. She slipped down to the living room. The only light was the glow of the silent TV. Mum sat on the couch. Lucie was lying on her lap, producing loud screams punctuated by gulping noises. Mum's hair looked punk. There was a long dribble of milk down her dressing gown, and her eyes were closed.

Jessica snuggled in beside her. "Oh, Jessica. Did Lucie

wake you? She's been fed, she's been burped, she's been changed, and she's been walked all over this house. I've run out of ideas." Jessica reached over and picked up the baby. It was like picking up a piece of wood. She propped her up over her shoulder and rubbed little circles on her back. Lucie cried on. Jessica's feet were still hot, so she took them out to the cool tile of the kitchen. She began to dance with Lucie, a circle dance she'd learned in school.

Side, behind, side, behind, step, kick. Like a needle being lifted from a record, Lucie stopped crying. Jessica hummed softly, circling the kitchen, and feeling the baby go heavier and softer in her arms. Mum leaned against the doorway. "Jessica, you are a genius."

After a week or so of pick-up meals, of take-out food and tuna melts from the toaster oven, Dad put his foot down. "This gastronomic chaos cannot continue," he declared. "We need a balanced meal with all the food groups represented, and we need to eat it all together at a table. With cutlery. Tomorrow I'm going to barbecue. Six o'clock. Be there."

Rowan turned up. Simon removed his Walkman. Even Lucie cooperated. She had just been fed and was seated in her plastic cuddle seat in the middle of the picnic table, where she kicked her feet and made little noises like a musical centerpiece. Jessica found it hard to concentrate on her hamburger and salad. It was more fun to play games with Lucie. "Alligator soup, alligator soup," she recited, "if I don't get some I think I'm going to . . ."

"Poop," said Simon.

"It's not poop. It's DROOP."

"It's poop to me," said Simon, stirring the mustard and ketchup around on his hamburger with his finger.

Jessica decided to ignore him. "Alligator pie," she continued. Lucie made a little gurgle. "Alligator pie, if I don't get some . . ."

"I won't zip up my fly," said Simon through a mouth full of potato salad.

"SIMON. That's gross. Dad, make Simon stop."

"There are limits, son," said Dad mildly. "Especially at dinner."

"Yes," said Mum. "And Simon, what are you doing with your hamburger?"

"I'm eating it," said Simon, not looking up.

Jessica saw Dad shoot a warning look at Mum but she didn't catch it. "Is it absolutely necessary to muck your food into a mess before you eat it?"

No answer.

"Simon, I asked you a question."

"Aw, lay off. What difference does it make?" Simon swung one leg over the bench.

"Simon, you haven't been excused from the table."

Silence came down over the picnic like a cloud on the mountains. Jessica played piano exercises on Lucie's toes.

Suddenly into the silence exploded the loudest burp Jessica had ever heard. All eyes turned to the centerpiece. Lucie bubbled softly.

And equally suddenly, everyone began to laugh. Giggles and bellylaughs and guffaws rang out into the yard. Bits of hamburger flew out of Simon's mouth. Dad gave one of his famous snorts, followed up an agonized "mayonnaise up my nose, help." Rowan barked like a seal and slapped the table. Mum sat with streaming eyes and a bright red face. Jessica held her stomach and tried to think of something sad. The laugh took on a life of its own, rising and falling until they were laughing at the laughter and then laughing at themselves laughing at the laughter. And through it all, Lucie sat like a tiny calm Buddha as if to say, "It is no more attention than I deserve."

Then it was over. When people had blown their noses on their paper napkins and mopped their eyes on the ends of their shirts, Jessica looked around the table and marveled at everyone's real face. It was as though everyone had washed off their make-up. Why can't we be like this always, she wondered.

Mum didn't have the open look that often. Mostly she looked closed in and tired. It was strange having her home in the day. Jessica remembered when she was in first grade and had longed for Mum to stay home like Cherry's mum did. And here it was, like a wish in a fairy story, but it wasn't quite what Jessica had expected. When Mum sat quietly nursing Lucie, it was perfect. But doing housework she was too fast and cranky.

A few days after the laughing picnic Jessica wandered into the kitchen where Mum was ironing in a mad way. It made Jessica glad she wasn't a shirt.

"Hey, Mum, what's for dinner?"

"Jessica Ruth Robertson, it's only 3:30 in the afternoon. How should I know what's for dinner?"

Jessica felt tears well up in her eyes. "Oh."

Mum looked up. "Oh, Jess, I'm sorry. I've just had it, what with being up all night with Lucie. I had forgotten how babies can't tell you what's wrong. It was *such* a relief when all of you learned to talk. And parts of being home are so *boring*. Tired and bored is a bad combination. What did your dad *do* all day when he was home?"

Jessica knew the question didn't really require an answer, but she answered anyway. "He ironed spiders into the pillowcases."

"He *what?*"

"He ironed spiders into the pillowcases. Look." Jessica grabbed a pillowcase from the pile and picked up the iron. "First you iron it flat, like usual. Then you iron it into four. Then you iron corner to corner, corner to corner. Then you turn up a little bit at the center and iron across. Then you open it out and *voilà*, a spider."

"Jessica, how often did your father do this?"

"Every time. Every Saturday night, on bed-changing day, I had a spider on my pillowcase. I've always had one. Didn't he do that to your pillowcases?"

"He certainly did NOT. What a waste of time. That's just RIDICULOUS. Novelty ironing. As if ironing didn't take enough time. REALLY. Ironing insects into pillowcases."

Jessica thought of mentioning that spiders weren't

insects, but it didn't seem the right time. Mum was carrying on.

"If you think I'm about to do that, FORGET IT. And I hope you don't think that you should learn to do this, Jessica. There are more important things in LIFE to learn, you know, there are MORE . . ."

". . . Mum. MUM. Don't get mad. Listen. I don't want *you* to iron like Dad. *I* don't want to iron like Dad. I was just telling you about it."

"Well. All right. As long as you REALIZE that."

This was silly. Jessica felt like she was having an argument with Margaret.

Then it hit her. Mum was not acting like an adult. She was being as stubborn, as irritable, as plain old stupid as any kid. After all, fancy ironing was just a joke.

Then a second thought hit Jessica like a wave that knocks you off your feet. Mum didn't understand jokes. She was smart and strong and neat and beautiful. But she didn't understand jokes.

Jessica looked at Mum and felt as though she was seeing a new person. Suddenly it felt not as though Mum were a kid, but as though she, Jessica, were a grown-up. The thought filled her with a bouncing naughtiness.

"Hey, Mum."

"Yes."

"Did you know that Dad makes pancakes in the shape of animals on Sunday mornings? Will you do that on Sunday?"

Mum flipped the iron up with a crash. "Jessica, I cannot do everything the way your father does."

"Mum."

"Yes."

"I was just kidding."

"What?"

"About the pancakes. Dad doesn't do that. I read it in a cookbook. I just wanted to bug you."

"Oh." Mum picked up an armload of sheets and hesitated, giving Jessica a long look. Then she grinned, "Well, in that case, Jessica Ruth Robertson, you are an unspeakable NERD!" With these words Mum threw all the sheets onto Jessica's head.

Jessica inhaled the perfume of washed sheets with a sigh of contentment. That was all right then. She was halfway up the stairs when the doorbell rang.

"Jess, get that, will you?"

Jessica jumped from the seventh step.

"Jessica, don't crash."

Standing at the door was a policeman. He was very wide and seemed to fill the whole doorway. "Is this the home of Mrs. Susan Robertson?"

"Who is it, Jess?" Mum's voice floated in from the kitchen.

"Just a minute," said Jessica. "I'll get her." But Mum arrived in the hall, carrying an armload of laundry.

"Are you Mrs. Susan Robertson?"

"Yes. What's the matter?"

"Are you the owner of a 1980 Toyota Tercel license JAWS?"

"Oh, well, that's really my sons, you see. They bought me a vanity license plate for my birthday. A joke, you know . . ." Mum's voice trailed off.

The policeman cleared his throat. "Did you fill up your car with gas at the Esso self-serve at 4th and Burrard at approximately 9:30 this morning?"

"Oh, yes, I was on my way to the doctor's. I was taking the baby for a . . . oh, cripes." Mum dropped the laundry on the hall table. "I didn't pay, did I? I had this feeling as I was driving away that I had forgotten something, but I thought it was the gas cap so I stopped farther down the street to check and that was okay so I forgot about it. Oh, I'm terribly sorry."

Mum wasn't speaking in capital letters. In fact, her words seemed to be getting smaller and smaller. The policeman replied as though he had memorized his speech. "The service station does not intend to press charges, ma'am, if you settle this matter as soon as possible."

"Oh, I will. I definitely will. Jessica, get my purse, will you? Oh, my goodness, how embarrassing. I'll go right away and pay and apologize. Jessica, *find my purse.*"

"Don't know where it is."

At this moment Lucie woke up and gave her opera singer yell. The back door slammed and Simon's voice boomed out, "Hey, what's going on? How come there's a cop car in front of the house?" He burst in from the kitchen.

"Simon, *go away*. Jessica, get Lucie. *I'll* find my purse."

Finally Lucie was quieted and the purse was found and coffee was offered to the policeman who declined, but it seemed to take forever. When the door finally shut behind him, Mum gave a great sigh and sat down on the stairs with Lucie in her arms.

"What was all that about?" Simon emerged from the kitchen with a jug of milk in his hand.

When Mum began to tell the story, Simon's face lit up. "If you had been put in jail we would have had to come and talk to you through little wire screens."

"Yes," said Jessica, "and you would have had to wear black and white striped clothes."

"Better practice rattling a tin cup against the bars," said Simon.

They went on like this until they had said everything they could think of about prison life. "Now seriously," said Mum. "I don't think we need to tell your father about this.

But of course they did have to tell Dad. At dinner Simon kept saying things like, "I guess you're really enjoying dinner, eh, Mum? Better than bread and water, eh? And it must be a treat to eat from dishes, I guess"— until Dad demanded an explanation.

And so the story was told again, and it got a bit better. "So the policeman, who was about as big as the door, said, 'Does Jaws live here . . .' "

"A life of crime," said Dad. "I think maybe you need

some rehabilitation. Would you like to go out to dinner? Just you and me. No children?"

"I'm not a child," mumbled Simon.

"Oh, sorry. No, um, descendants?"

"You mean to a proper restaurant? You mean where we will get to hear some music other than 'Sweat Socks' and 'Charlene'? You mean where people will come and put lovely food in front of us? What a good idea. What will we do about Lucie?"

"I think the three other childr . . . I mean, offspring, could babysit for an evening. How about tomorrow?"

"Not me," said Simon, as the sullen look crept back onto his face. "I've got a game."

"Jess, go phone the bagman and see if he can come."

7

So the preparations for baby-sitting began. Jessica went to the library the next day and got out a "Baby-sitters' Guide." She spent the afternoon filling out checklists.

"Does this child have any food allergies?"

"We don't really know, Jessica. All she has ever had is breastmilk." Jessica filled in "not known."

"Now, Jessica, I'll feed her before I go and I'll leave a bottle of milk. Give it to her if she's fussy. She'll probably sleep the whole time."

Not if I have anything to do with it, thought Jessica.

"We'll be home by ten," said Mum.

"Don't hurry."

At five o'clock Rowan arrived with a pizza and a video player and two movies. "Come on, kid. Let's make a night of it."

"Have a good time," said Mum. "What are you going to watch?"

"*Mary Poppins* and a documentary on life in the Arctic," said Rowan. Mum looked surprised. She gave a lot more instructions until Dad finally pulled her out the door.

Rowan took the pizza out of its insulated bag (exclusive bagman design) and he and Jessica sat on the couch with Lucie between them. Jessica carefully picked the anchovy off her wedge.

"What's the matter? Don't you like anchovies yet?" Rowan was winding mozzarella around his finger.

"What do you mean 'yet'? I don't like anchovies. I never did and I never will. Why do grown-ups always think that when you don't like something, you'll learn to like it later. That's just kidism."

Rowan looked thoughtful. "Yeah. Good point. I don't figure I'm going to learn to like parsnips. Next time I'll order your half anchovy-free. Anyway, hurry up, okay? There's something I want to do with Lucie before she goes to sleep."

"What?"

"Pictures. Dan lent me this great Polaroid camera, so I can keep a record of the bags I make. But I'd rather take baby pictures."

Jessica gulped the rest of her pizza and Rowan got the camera ready. They started out with regular pictures— Lucie and her pink stuffed dog, Lucie on her sheepskin, Lucie propped in the big armchair. Then Rowan tried out some artsy angles—an aerial view down onto the top of Lucie's head, a view of the bottom of her feet. They waited for each picture to appear, darkening and clearing as Lucie appeared out of the mist.

"It's kind of like she's being born, isn't it?" whispered Jessica.

Then Rowan spotted Simon's ugly peaked cap on the hook in the hall and they got silly. Soon, propped along the windowsill were a line of Lucie pictures. Lucie under an umbrella, Lucie peeking from behind the palm tree, Lucie reading *Journal of Engineering Science*, Lucie wearing a Walkman, Lucie with a nasturtium behind her ear. Even Lucie in the fruit bowl, held in place by an invisible Jessica.

Finally Rowan ran out of film and Lucie drifted quietly off to sleep. Jessica held her while Rowan put on the video. The opening scene was of a giant black motorcycle roaring off the edge of a cliff.

"What happened to *Mary Poppins?*" asked Jessica.

Rowan winked. "What they don't know won't hurt them. This is called *Kawasaki Kamakazis*. And wait until you see the second one. It's *Attack of the Killer Pomegranates*. Great lichee nut scene."

"Wow," said Jessica. She would really have preferred Jane and Michael Banks and "Feed the Birds," but with brothers you sometimes had to pretend to be grosser than you were.

Around the scene where the motorcycles blasted across

a rope bridge that was hanging by one strand over a river of piranhas, Jessica slipped away to the kitchen to heat up a bottle. She tested its temperature against the inside of her wrist. Then she returned to the living room where a biker was meeting a watery death and picked up Lucie.

Upstairs Jessica sat on the rocker in Lucie's dimly lit room. A few whimpers later, Lucie was happily drinking, one hand hanging on to Jessica's finger. Jessica softly sang "Ninety-Nine Bottles of Beer on the Wall" and by the time she reached forty-two, the milk was all gone. Simon banged through the front door and began to talk to Rowan.

For burping, Jessica sang the ABC song, followed by as much as she could remember of the books of the Bible. One year at camp a dull girl named Narene had amazed everyone at talent night by a musical rendition of the books of the Bible. All Jessica could remember was up to Joshua, so she sang that a few times until Lucie was thoroughly burped and asleep again.

Jessica put her into the crib. The moon shone through the venetian blinds, throwing bands of silver across the baby's downy head. Jessica ran her finger lightly down the center of Lucie's face, forehead to chin, and inhaled the warm smell of sleeping baby.

"Lucie," she whispered. Lucie breathed on, the bear appliqué on her sleeper barely visible as it rose and fell. She shifted and made a sucking shape with her mouth. Did babies dream, Jessica wondered. She thought of how when

Ollie purred in her sleep Dad always said, "She's dreaming of ancient Egypt." But if babies didn't know words and couldn't talk and everything was new, what was the difference between waking and sleeping? Jessica tried to think of something she could wish for Lucie and talk into her dream. Finally she laid her spread-out hand on Lucie's chest and whispered, "Be happy."

Then she crouched down and rested her head against the bars of the crib until her feet got pins and needles. She found that the quietness of the baby had got inside her and she didn't want lights and television and loud brothers, so she crept along to the bathroom and brushed her teeth in the dark. Then she went to put on her pajamas.

On her way back downstairs to say goodnight to the boys, she overheard someone in Lucie's room. She stopped outside to listen. It was Simon. He was reading aloud.

"The transverse-mounted fuel-injected four produces one hundred twelve pound-feet of torque at forty-eight thousand r.p.m., and virtually every ounce of that is useable because of an improved five-speed gearbox."

Why, that rat, thought Jessica. He teases me for reading and singing to the baby and now he's doing the same thing. She tiptoed downstairs to tell Rowan.

"Shhh," Rowan held up his hand. "This is the very best part. See that guy? He's a triple agent disguised as a fruit wholesaler and he's about to expose the whole banana scandal."

"Rowan, guess what Simon is doing."

"What?" Rowan's eyes did not stray from the screen.

"He's up there reading *Motor Trend* to Lucie."

No answer.

"ROW-an," Jessica tugged at his sleeve. "Simon is actually reading to Lucie. Let's go up and surprise him, okay?"

Rowan finally turned from the TV. "He's *reading* to Lucie?"

"Yeah. Something about engines. Come on, we can hide outside and listen and surprise him."

"No, Jess, let's not. He probably doesn't want us to know he's doing it."

"Of course he doesn't. That's the whole point."

"I just don't think we should go and embarrass him."

Jessica felt that she was being told off. She felt herself holding on tightly to her idea of Simon as a jerk, fighting off a new way of seeing him. But then she suddenly felt too tired to do much of anything. Her arms felt like they were dragging on the ground.

"I'm going to bed then."

Rowan reached out and rumpled Jessica's hair. "Sleep tight." For a second he looked and sounded just like Dad.

Jessica woke later to the now-familiar nighttime sound of Lucie crying. She cozied down in her bed with a feeling of family around her.

8

By noon the next day Jessica was more fed up with Simon than she had ever been before. He started off on the wrong foot with Dad by leaving wet towels all over the bathroom floor. And then when Mum asked how Lucie had been the night before, he said, "Aw, the little rug-rat was okay early but she cried all night again. Can't you give her drugs or something?"

Before she had time to stop herself, Jessica blurted out, "Yeah, well, she was probably having nightmares about gearboxes."

"What?" Simon's head jerked up and he gave Jessica a disgusted look.

"What are we talking about?" asked Dad.

Jessica mumbled into her cereal. "Nothing." She practiced floating one cornflake on a lake of milk, but she felt Mum and Dad look at each other over her head. She knew she had blown one more chance of being happy with Simon. But he shouldn't have called Lucie a rug-rat.

Dad's "Let's get up and at 'em" voice interrupted the sound of deliberate chewing. "Simon, would you like to mow the grass this morning?"

"No, I wouldn't *like* to. I will, but I won't *like* to. If you want me to do something, just ask me, don't say, 'would I like to.' "

Dad cleared his throat. "Come on, son. You wouldn't really prefer me to say, 'Simon, cut grass' (Dad put on a caveman voice), would you? It is just a figure of speech, after all."

Simon didn't reply but slammed out the door and Jessica heard him crashing around the carport getting out the lawn mower.

"Susan, were we really as awful as that at his age? I mean, I don't say anything about his music or his room . . ."

"It's the process of individuation, David. Painful but normal."

"Oh, yeah, that. Well, I just wish he would get it over with."

Mum continued, "Anyway, he does have a point about Lucie's crying. Of course, all babies do it, but that's one of those memories I'd blocked out. Maybe we should get one of those tapes that sound like the womb. You know, Monique at the prenatal class talked about them."

Dad snorted. "You mean weird Monique? She was the

one who wanted a recording of whales to be played during delivery, wasn't she?"

"What does the womb sound like?" asked Jessica.

"It's kind of a swooshing sound, like waves on the shore."

"Anyway," said Dad, "crying is not supposed to be bad for babies. It can just be exercise, after all." Just at that moment a voice drifted up the hot air register.

"Like two socks from the dryer
We used to stick together,
But you left me for another
And I'm living cling-free.
Cling-free, cling-free,
That's the way it's gonna be,
Cause you left me for another
And I'm living cling-free."

"Oh, help," said Dad, burying his face in a napkin.

As Jessica left the kitchen she felt an idea coming on. She went to phone Margaret. Margaret saw the potential right away and rushed over. Together they gathered everything they needed.

"It's going to be a surprise," said Jessica, "so we'll have to do some sneaking."

First they went into the broom cupboard to find a handle that screwed off. But none did. "We'll just have to take the whole sponge mop, then," said Jessica. They found string and elastic bands in the junk drawer. Then they mucked around in the tapes sitting by the stereo. The tapes were a mess—crossed-out, whited-out, relabeled. Finally they found one that said "Banjo Instruction" on side A and "Romantic Organ Moods" on side B, but when they tried it out, it seemed blank.

"Okay, Margaret," said Jessica. "Now comes the hard part. We have to steal Simon's tape recorder."

"Why don't we just ask to borrow it? After all, he lent it to us before."

"Well, there isn't a chance he would lend it to me today. He's not even speaking to me. Here's what we have to do. I'm going to sneak into his room to get it. You stand guard on the stairs. If he comes, you make a noise like an owl, okay?"

With Margaret on the stairs and the reassuring whir of the lawn mower outside, Jessica got up enough courage to enter Simon's room. She stood at the doorway for a second, looking at the mess.

Every surface was covered with stuff, with toppling piles of paper and magazines and with heaps of tangled clothes. The desk had a complicated set of dusty plastic pipes and test tubes from some old chemistry project. The unmade bed was covered with newspapers, on which there seemed to be a dismantled bicycle. On the walls the posters were half falling down, and around the edge of the ceiling was a single yellowing vine resting on hooks—Simon's attempt to grow the longest houseplant in the world.

Finally Jessica spied a corner of the tape recorder poking out from under a pair of ski boots. She edged it out without disturbing the surface mess and fled, grabbing a beach towel from the linen closet to wrap it in.

Margaret stowed the wrapped tape recorder in her bike basket and Jessica tied the sponge mop across her handlebars.

Just as they were pulling out of the garage they heard Dad. "You going out to be cleaning women?"

Jessica jumped. "Er, no, I'm just using it for something down at the beach."

"Oh, yes, cleaning up the beach. Good idea. Just remember to bring back the mop when you're finished."

They biked down past the crowded part of the beach to the wilder strip. Jessica thought of how much better the beach was in winter or in the rain. People at the beach on an overcast day were the best sort of people. Some had dogs. Some had machines that find coins and valuables lost in the sand. There were fast walkers, or old people who sat all bundled up on benches and read.

In the winter you could look for shells and good bits of wood. You could draw pictures in the sand when the tide went out. In the winter people said hello to you when they passed you. In the winter you had to take your own snacks and you could ride your bike along the no-biking paths and hardly ever get caught. Water ran down the cliffs in winter, all slick and greasy, and sometimes you saw herons.

But in May the bulldozers came in and raked the sand and the place wasn't yours any more. In the summer, the beach was different. No dogs allowed. Bike riding only on the bike path. Towels lined up against each other like a patchwork quilt. In the summer you couldn't even read properly on the beach without squinting. And the herons never came.

The only hope in summer was to go a bit farther to the rocky part of the beach where there was no life-guard. Real things happened on this part of the beach. Sometimes at twilight men in hip waders walked out into the bay and set up nets for smelt fishing. And you could catch crabs off the end of the wharf.

Jessica and Margaret biked beyond the wharf to a secluded rocky place. "Perfect," said Jessica.

"There's one thing I don't get," said Margaret. "We're going to make a tape recording of waves to put Lucie to sleep, right?"

"Right."

"And she'll like it because it will be like the sounds of the womb, right?"

"Right."

"But before Lucie was born we made sure that she heard the encyclopedia and great composers. Shouldn't that put her to sleep? Why don't we record that?"

"But that was for when she was awake. We want something for when she was asleep."

"You mean she was awake and asleep in there?"

"Of course, what did you think?" Jessica was suddenly not at all sure about this.

"I don't know. I thought she was sort of half-awake all the time."

"Anyway, some mother at the prenatal class told Mum about this and how it really works, so let's get started."

Jessica attached the microphone to the non-sponge end of the mop with elastic bands. "Okay, here's what we do. I'll hold this microphone out over the waves and you turn on the tape recorder. Now you have to be really careful to put on the pause button really quick if there's any other kind of noise, like a truck or somebody yelling. Let's try it."

Jessica held the sponge-mop out over the waves and Margaret crouched with the tape recorder on the rocks. "Ready, set, roll'em," said Margaret.

It all took a lot longer than they had expected. First a man came along with a huge radio and Margaret forgot to stop the tape. Then they discovered that every time they pushed the pause button the tape went "vwip." But the biggest problem was that the waves just weren't loud enough as they gently lapped up on the sand.

"I think we need to be on a surfing beach or something," said Jessica. "This isn't working."

Margaret had a solution. "If the waves aren't big enough, let's just make them bigger. I'll go out in the water with a flat board and push the water up in waves. Look, let's put some rocks right here. In the movies, it's always the waves crashing up against rocks."

Margaret ended up getting a bit wet, but it seemed to

work. They rolled barnacle-covered boulders down to the edge of the water and then Margaret waded out. It was a gentle slope, so she had to go quite a way. When she pushed the water onto the boulders, it made a convincing sound. But this meant that Jessica had to hold the microphone out and work the tape recorder at the same time. So she took off one running shoe, balanced the tape recorder on a flat part of the rock, held out the microphone as far as she could and worked the on/off button with her toe.

"Okay," said Margaret. "Roll'em, this is a take."

Then everything happened at once. Margaret gave a huge heave with her board. The wave approached the rocks. Jessica reached out with one toe to push the on button and her foot slid on a seaweed-slimy part of the rock and she fell off. She managed not to knock off the tape recorder, at the cost of a barnacle-scraped leg. But she couldn't keep hold of the sponge mop.

Margaret saw what was happening and lunged to grab the microphone before it hit the water. She disappeared beneath the seaweed just as the microphone did. She emerged, flicking water out of her eyes and holding the sponge mop and microphone aloft.

Jessica was bloody. Margaret was soaked. They took the microphone apart and tried to dry the pieces with the towel. But when they put it together again all it did was hiss.

"What are you going to do?" Margaret asked.

"I'm going to go home and tell Simon what I've done

and say I'm sorry and say I'm going to have the micro-phone repaired."

"Really?"

"No. I can't do it. He hates me already. If he knows I've done this he'll never speak to me again for the rest of my life."

"I could say I did it. It doesn't matter if Simon doesn't speak to me for the rest of my life."

"Thanks, but it doesn't help. I'm the one who took it without permission. I'm not even supposed to be in his room."

When Jessica got home, Mum was sitting in the living room nursing Lucie. "Hi, Mum. Simon here?" Jessica tried to sound casual.

"No, he's still over at Patrick's, I think."

Jessica went upstairs and tiptoed into Simon's room. She put the tape recorder right back under the ski boots. Then she cleaned her leg up.

Downstairs she cuddled up to Mum on the couch. Lucie smacked and slurped.

"What did you and Margaret do at the beach?"

"We tried to make some waves with a board and Margaret fell in and then I scraped my leg on some barnacles."

"When I was your age they used to say that sea water was good for cuts, but it stung like mad. Of course now it probably isn't, what with pollution. Did you wash it out?"

"Yup." Jessica tried to catch Mum's quiet mood, but she felt twitchy and unsettled. "Mum, I think Simon hates me."

"Oh, Jessica, he doesn't. It's just a difficult time for him right now. You'll be friends again soon."

"But how do you know?"

"Because he was such a funny little guy." Mum looked out over Lucie's head. "Go and get the photo box, would you?"

Jessica rooted around the hall cupboard and came up with a cardboard box tied with string, the nearest thing the family had to a photo album. Mum began to flip through the pictures. "When he's obnoxious now, I remind myself how loving he was as a little boy." She pulled out a photo of the totem poles in Stanley Park. "Look at this one. Dad was going through his Indian art phase then and we spent a lot of time visiting totem poles. Simon thought that the figures on the poles were ugly and he felt sorry for them, so he always wanted to kiss them. Dad would lift him up onto his shoulders to reach the high faces. I think Lucie's finished. Here, burp her, would you? I'm going to get a diaper."

Jessica propped the milk-smelling Lucie over her shoulder and rubbed a vigorous circle on her back. Lucie burped and threw up a little. "Yuck," said Jessica. Mum changed Lucie and put her down in the pram by the front door. Then she turned to the photo box again.

"Here it is." She pulled out a slightly blurry photo of herself and Simon and Rowan. Rowan was looking like Christopher Robin with a cap of hair and short pants. Simon stood with his chin stuck out, his shirt untucked, and his hair sticking up in spikes.

"What's Simon holding?"

"That's Ollie, dressed up in your baby clothes. Simon got so impatient for you to be born that we had to get him a kitten. I think Rowan put him up to dressing her in your bonnet and sweater."

"Where am I?"

Mum grinned and pointed to the billowy peasant dress she was wearing in the picture. "You're in there."

Jessica looked hard at the picture. Mum's face looked the same, but her hair was black. "You mean I'm not born yet?"

"Right. You arrived a couple of weeks later. Ollie was sure glad. Simon was so ga-ga about you that he started to ignore the cat."

"What do you mean?"

"Simon adored you. He wouldn't let anyone near you unless he gave the go-ahead. He announced your arrival to everyone—people on buses, the Safeway checker. And he wanted you to talk right away. I caught him one day when you were about three weeks old. He was holding up a magazine to your face and saying, 'Cow, say it. Cow.'"

"Why didn't you ever tell me this before?"

"I don't know. I sort of forgot. Lucie brings it all back."

Jessica suddenly felt as though she didn't know her family at all. Then Lucie woke up and began to wail.

"Can I take her for a walk? She'll stop crying if she's moving."

"Sure, that would be a great help."

Jessica took Lucie on a graph paper walk. Up a block,

across a block, up a block, across a block, thinking about a young black-haired woman with Mum's face and a little boy kissing totem poles. She looked down at Lucie. Ga-ga? That was a good way of describing how she felt when Lucie gurgled.

Jessica had just got home and was sitting in the living room when Simon got back. She heard his every step on the way to his room. Would he notice? She hid in the corner of the couch and read her book like mad when he came downstairs and started mooching around at the stereo. But Simon didn't notice her. He left an untidy heap of tapes and cassette boxes on the floor and went upstairs again. There was the sound of things being moved around.

At dinner Simon said, "Has anyone seen my 'Sweat Socks' tape?"

"Where did you leave it?" asked Mum.

Simon put on his mock-patient look. "If I knew where I left it, I would know where it was."

Dad looked up with a warning expression. "Have you looked at that pile of tapes in the living room?"

"Yeah, and I was sure it was there. It's a tape I made from Patrick's record."

"Was it labeled?"

"Yeah, it was labeled 'Banjo Instruction.'"

Jessica gulped. "In a blue cover?" Simon nodded. She had to say it now before she thought about it. "I took it."

Simon made an angry clicking sound on the roof of his mouth. "Well, where is it?"

"I taped over it."

"Hey, it took me an hour to make that tape. Why don't you leave my stuff alone?"

"But it didn't seem like there was anything on the tape. I checked."

"What do you need tapes for, anyway?"

"Just something."

"You're always getting into my stuff. You're always wrecking it. Why don't you just keep out of it?"

"Okay," said Mum, "before you fly off the handle. I know you're disappointed to have your tape lost, but I think if it wasn't labeled properly and Jessica did try, then she isn't really to blame. How about if you buy Simon a new blank tape, Jessica? Then we'll call it even. I'm sure Patrick would let you tape his record again, Simon. And this time label it properly and keep it in your room."

"Yeah, okay. I'm . . . I'm sorry I got mad."

Mum opened her mouth but Dad put his hand out to cover hers and spoke very quickly. "So, anyone for ice cream?"

Jessica stirred her ice cream around till it melted. So Simon had actually apologized. Dad was in the right. Simon was in the right. Mum was in the right. She was in the right. Everything settled. Nobody holding on to being mad. Except. How could she ever tell Simon about the microphone now?

9

*J*essica didn't usually get very much mail. She had a pen pal in Australia, but once they had exchanged a few letters about families, pets, school, and how funny it was that it was summer there when it was winter here, the correspondence petered out. For a while Jessica sent away a lot of coupons to receive brochures on hotels in Mazatlan or pamphlets on feeding jelly to your houseplants, but Mum made her stop. "We get enough junk mail around here already."

Dad understood more about wanting mail, and he gave Jessica two magazine subscriptions for Christmas. But letters were still rare. So she was surprised to find a letter on her desk when she came home one day. It was addressed in several colors of felt-tip marker and on the back was written, "Dear Letter Carrier, thank you for your prompt and courteous delivery of this letter." That was a dead giveaway. Only one person would think of thanking the letter carrier. Cherry Dorkley, whose father was a mailman.

Inside was an invitation to a birthday sleep-over at Cherry's. It was a picture of a unicorn with big eyes and long eyelashes. A word balloon coming out of its mouth said, "Come with me to a Mythical Land." In the background were pictures of ladies in long gowns with cones on their heads and men in armor. Inside it said, "Oh, ladies of the court, you are cordially invited to a fête to help celebrate the festival of Lady Cherry Dorkley's eleventh year."

Typical, thought Jessica. Every year Cherry had a theme party. Cherry's mum wrote a column for the neighborhood paper called "Perk Up a Party" and she really did. In fact, Cherry's mum tried to perk up everything. Christmas at their house was like something out of a magazine. The year before, Mrs. Dorkley had done angels. There were angels on the perfect tree, angels on all the wrapping paper, angels stenciled on the windows, and a flood-lit angel on the roof.

Jessica looked over the invitation again. At least it didn't mention a magician. Last year's theme had been rainbows. Not only were there rainbows everywhere—on the cake, on the party hats, on the tablecloth, on the napkins, fancy sandwiches with blue bread and pink and green cream cheese—but there was also a magician who pulled rainbows out of hats.

Jessica hated magicians. As far as she was concerned, magicians were all part of some nasty game of trying to put other people down by fooling them. Besides, last year's magician had smelled like old cigarettes.

In spite of Mrs. Dorkley's column in the paper, nobody else in the neighborhood perked up their parties. Mostly everyone had the same party. Dinner at McDonald's, a video movie, cake and ice cream and then a sleep-over. At the sleep-over everybody stayed awake as long as possible talking about what teachers were really like, and how it would feel to live in someone else's body.

To tell the truth, the regular kind of party was best. At Cherry's parties her mum was always hanging around to make sure you were having a good time, and every minute was organized. It was kind of like summer camp.

Cherry's eleventh birthday was no exception. The six girls arrived to find Cherry sitting on a big chair in the dining room. The chair was decorated to look like a throne. She looked lonely. Then Mrs. Dorkley made them put on their nightgowns and gave each girl a tall paper cone with some gauze stuck on the top and some jewelry to wear. The dining room was hung with bath towels. "Tapestries," Cherry sighed. On the long table were candles in all sorts of holders. At each seat was a place card done in funny writing. Jessica's said, "Jeffica."

For dinner they had mead (strawberry Kool Aid),

bread that they ripped off a big loaf, and chicken legs. Margaret pretended to be Henry VIII and threw her bones over her shoulder when she had finished. "Here, Fido!" But they hit the curtain and made a grease spot. Mrs. Dorkley wasn't pleased.

The cake was shaped like a castle with pennants and a little drawbridge made out of chocolate.

After dessert they played "Pin the horn on the unicorn." This was quite boring and made worse by Mr. Dorkley filming the whole thing on videotape. Mrs. Dorkley once wrote a column called "Capture the Memories," and each year she kept a scrapbook for Cherry's birthday with the invitation, the place card and lots of pictures.

Jessica hated having her picture taken. It made her face freeze. But being videotaped was worse.

Things got a bit better when they played "Pass the Parcel." The girls sat in a circle and Mrs. Dorkley put on a record of Walt Disney's "The Reluctant Dragon." As long as the music was on, the girls passed a parcel round and round. As soon as the music stopped, the person with the parcel ripped off as many of the layers of paper as she could before the music started again. Mr. Dorkley took the video camera to the top of a stepladder to get some special effects.

The girls were well-behaved for the first few rounds, but then the parcel stopped at Margaret. She played to win, ripping and roaring and using her teeth. From then on it was loud and wild. Mrs. Dorkley started to look worried.

Everybody lost their cone hats and Cherry got the giggles so badly she started to choke. Mr. Dorkley stopped filming.

After "Pass the Parcel" (Lisa won—it was a green fuzzy-felt dragon), Mrs. Dorkley poured herself a big glass of wine and went upstairs to her room. The girls went down to the basement where there were foam mats all over the floor. Then came the best part. Mr. Dorkley said they could use the video camera to make a movie if they liked.

Everyone had an idea. Miranda was in favor of making a soap opera, but everyone else said there was too much talking in a soap opera. Holly had an idea for a horror movie, but Cherry worried about getting ketchup on the furniture. Margaret favored a hard-hitting documentary. "Let's blow the cover on the sock industry. They could make socks that last forever, but do they? No. The sock companies just keep this super-sock a secret so that we all have to go and buy new socks all the time."

Carly wanted to do "Stars of Tomorrow" so that she could demonstrate her modern jazz dance routine. But Cherry wanted to do a program on the lives of the rich and famous. At first this didn't appeal to anyone but, after all, as she reminded them, it was her house and her party. And the idea got better and better.

Margaret decided to be director and scriptwriter and camerawoman. She made a clapper board out of the slate from Cherry's schoolroom kit and a wooden spoon, held together with elastic bands.

The first segment was of Holly wearing Cherry's bathing suit to do aerobic exercises to music, and saying how important it was to keep your body in shape, especially when you were extremely rich. "It's a take," said Margaret. "Put it in the can."

Then Jessica dressed up one of Cherry's dolls. The doll wore everybody's jewels and Jessica pretended to be the mother of the richest baby in the world. "Yes, my baby has a solid gold crib and a solid gold playpen and a solid gold teething ring and satin diapers. She has eighty-seven thousand piggy banks filled with money but really, she just wants the simple life."

Lisa and Carly got silly when it was their turn to be rich movie stars, but Margaret made them shape up. "Take three," she said. "This is for real."

Cherry tied a scarf around her neck to be a TV interviewer. "Here we are on the set of Rambo Seventeen, speaking with its stars . . ."

Around midnight they had the showing. First forward, then fast forward to hear themselves sound like chipmunks and look like crazy people, then with pauses for each person to study herself, then forward again.

"Hey," said Margaret. "What should we do now?" But Lisa and Carly were asleep and Holly was yawning inside her mouth and Jessica felt grit in her eyes. "I guess we should brush our teeth," said Cherry in a soft sleepy voice, but nobody did.

In the middle of the night, Jessica woke up. Her head

was at a funny angle. For a minute she couldn't remember where she was, and for a minute after that she felt lonely and a bit scared.

She sat up and listened to the breathing all around her. There was a lump under her feet. She leaned over and dug it out. It was Cherry's doll, lying where they had dropped her after the rich and famous. Jessica took off all the jewelry and smoothed down her dress. She laid her on the pillow beside her and went back to sleep. Later on, she was to think that this was the last time she had ever been happy all through.

Jessica woke up to an unfamiliar voice. "Jessica, Jessica." It was Mr. Dorkley. "Jessica, your dad has come to get you."

What was he doing there so early? What was he doing there at all? The questions bubbled up in Jessica's mind, but something about the look on Mr. Dorkley's face stopped them. She gathered her things together and stumbled into the bathroom. She put on her shorts and T-shirt, stuffed everything into her bag, stepped over the sleeping girls, and went upstairs.

Dad was sitting in the living room holding a mug of coffee. And it was the weirdest thing. Mr. Dorkley was standing behind him with his hand on Dad's shoulder. Mr. Dorkley didn't even know Dad. What was going on?

Dad looked as though his face would never move. He hadn't shaved and he was wearing old track pants and a shirt of Rowan's that said "Labatt's Six Mile Run." He grabbed Jessica's hand hard. It hurt, but Jessica knew she mustn't pull away. They walked to the door. Mr. Dorkley said, "If there's anything . . . just let us know."

Outside it was raining, the fine rain that just hangs in the air and touches your face so softly that you don't even realize you are getting wet.

Dad opened the car door. "Come on home, Jess."

Inside the car, Dad didn't start the motor. "Dad, what is it? Why are we going home?"

"Jessica, I have something very sad and hard to tell you. It's about Lucie."

Jessica looked straight ahead and saw the rain misting on the windshield. The outside world began to blur.

"She died, Jessica. She was up at two o'clock just fine and when Mum went in this morning she had stopped breathing. Mum gave her c.p.r. but it was too late. We don't know why it happened. It's called crib death and nobody really understands it."

"Stop," whispered Jessica. "Stop talking." And then she began to tremble. Dad reached out and pulled her to him. She felt as stiff and plastic as Cherry's doll.

They sat in silence. "We're going home now, Jess. Mum needs us."

On the drive home Jessica had only one thing in her head, the squeak of the windshield wiper. *Swish, squeak. Swish, squeak.* If it rained harder it wouldn't squeak so much. Jessica held onto this thought.

Everything on the way home looked exactly the same. Mrs. Gill ran by in her electric blue tracksuit. The stop sign on the corner still read "Stop—the Cruise." The sweet peas had reached the top of the trellis. The house dissolved and melted away but it was only because the wipers had been turned off.

Dad got out and pulled Jessica out after him on his side of the car. He held her around the shoulders as they walked inside the house.

10

When Jessica went inside, Mum and Simon were sitting in the kitchen and coffee was perking. Jessica had just a moment to think that it was early for Simon to be up before she was enfolded in a big silent hug.

Later on it seemed as though the week that followed Lucie's death was a video movie played on a machine with only two controls, fast forward and pause. Fast forward and pause, but no play, no record and, most of all, no rewind. In bed at night, scared of giving in to sleep, Jessica tried to rewind the tape to just before Lucie's death and then to make Lucie grow up. She tried to make her talk, and wear overalls, and walk down the street to her first day of kindergarten. But it didn't work. The pictures wouldn't come alive.

In the fast forward mode, Mum and Dad concentrated on finding Rowan. He was away wilderness camping. Nobody could remember who he was with or where they had gone.

"I think he went with Daniel."

"What's Daniel's last name?"

"I don't know but he works in that car wash on Broadway."

"What's it called?"

"I don't think it has a name."

They finally found out where he had planned to be and they phoned the Royal Canadian Mounted Police, who sent an officer out to give him a message.

When his van pulled up in the driveway, Jessica was leaning over the end of the couch looking out of the window. She watched him jump down from the driver's seat and slide open the rear door of the van. Suddenly—pause. He stopped with his hand on the door and rested his head against the side of the van. He doesn't want to come in, Jessica realized. As long as he doesn't come in the house, Lucie's death won't be real.

But he did come in, and things speeded up again. People came and went and all of them brought food—hams and casseroles and big cakes. Sometimes they just left the food on the porch. Charlene went home to visit her parents and came back with five dozen brown eggs. There were all kinds of long-distance phone calls. Nobody seemed to care how much they cost.

And then the cards started, more than at Christmas. There was even a card from Mr. Blackburn. It was signed, "Gerald Blackburn." Gerald? Jessica read all the cards carefully. But the words seemed strange. "A Brighter Tomorrow," "Beyond Life's Gateway," "The Rose Still Blooms Beyond the Wall." Hardly any of them used the words that were in Jessica's mind, like "death" and "sad."

Auntie Eileen flew out from Toronto. She arrived at midnight and first Mum was going to get her and then, no, she was going to take the airport bus and Dad was going to pick her up at the bus terminal and then Rowan was going to get her in the van and finally Mum went anyway.

Mum was the most fast forward of all—answering the phone, writing letters, making arrangements with the church. She talked to Jessica, explaining about crib death and including her in decisions. But Jessica remembered quiet moments snuggled against Mum as she nursed Lucie. She remembered standing with a pile of clean laundry on her head, feeling the rightness of everything. The rightness was gone. Part of Mum had gone.

In fast forward, things and people were sorted out. Auntie Eileen was going to sleep in Simon's room, so Simon was going to sleep in Jessica's room on an air mattress. Auntie Eileen couldn't use Simon's down comforter because she was allergic, so Jessica got to use it because she had the only other single bed blankets.

While everyone was getting ready for the funeral, the

ironing board was never put away. Rowan washed the car twice and Eileen and Dad made lots of fancy sandwiches and borrowed a coffee urn from the church.

And then, abruptly, the pause button was pushed.

Dad, with his head in the linen cupboard. "Look, I'm giving Eileen the orange towels and if either of you so much as *touch* them it'll be . . ."

Pause. Jessica knew what Dad had been about to say. His threat was always the same. He talked out of the side of his mouth like a gangster and said, "It'll be curtains for you." But this time he stopped and stumbled and finally said, "Well, just don't." Even words changed. Nothing could ever be the same. "Don't be such a baby." "He nearly died laughing."

One afternoon Auntie Eileen was sitting on the couch with her legs curled under her and Ollie on her lap. She looked at one of the Polaroid pictures of Lucie. "She kind of looked like a Sumo wrestler, didn't she?" Dad smiled and then the smile began to tremble. Pause. Auntie Eileen dumped Ollie, went to the kitchen, and came back with a box of Kleenex. She set it down on the coffee table in front of Dad.

That night Jessica woke up with a stomachache. She went down to the kitchen to get a glass of milk and there sat Simon. Pause. The single light over the table shone through his hair. He looked as if he was on stage. All over the table were piles of pennies and little purple packages. Simon's face didn't move. Only his hands. Ten, ten, ten,

ten, ten. Five groups of ten and none left over. He balanced the pennies on his long hand and slid them into a purple roll. He flicked down the ends. He began again.

And the funeral. All so fast and Jessica trying to concentrate on not crying. Catching glimpses of people in church—the next-door neighbors, Uncle Gordie, people from Mum's office, Margaret, Margaret's mother. All looking like strangers. And then on the way out, Simon grabbed her hand. Pause. Jessica looked up at him and he didn't look back. His jaw was set. But he kept her hand all the way to the back of the church.

Mum standing there speaking to everyone. "Thank you so much for coming. Thank you so much for coming. Yes, it means a lot to us. Give my fond regards to Bea. Thank you so much for coming." Until the words didn't mean anything at all.

After the funeral people came back to the house for tea and fancy sandwiches and pastries. It was just like a party but not like a party at all. Mum asked Jessica to pass things. She felt as though everyone was staring at her. Margaret helped pass.

When they went into the kitchen to fill the cream pitcher, Auntie Eileen took one look at them and said, "Hold it." She took a plate, loaded it with sandwiches, and handed it to Margaret. "Here. That's for you two. Beat it."

They sat on the floor in Jessica's room, leaning against the bed. Margaret picked at her one tuna salad on brown bread. Jessica rhythmically ate her way through fourteen sandwiches—peanut butter pinwheels, asparagus roll-ups, egg salad checkerboards.

"Don't you like maraschino and cream cheese?"

Margaret shook her head.

"I'll have it, then."

Finally Margaret spoke. "I'm going to miss Lucie."

The words rushed up in Jessica's throat. "Oh, Margaret, I don't think I'm ever going to be happy again."

Margaret squished the last of her sandwich into a pellet. "No, you won't," she said quietly. "I mean, you won't be this sad all the time, but you won't have that . . . happy in every part feeling." She turned slightly away from Jessica and looked toward the window. "Before my dad went away I thought everything could be fixed. I broke my collarbone on the monkey bars, but it got better. Dad and Mum had lots of fights, but they always made up. In kindergarten my best friend moved away at Christmas, and I thought I would never have another best friend. But I did." Margaret grabbed Jessica's hand but she didn't look at her. The inside of Jessica's nose began to itch. She looked up at the ceiling so the tears wouldn't spill over. Right now it was important to listen, not to cry. Margaret might never talk like this again.

"So when Dad went away I thought *that* could be fixed, too. I thought it could be fixed because all he had to do was come home. And he did, a few times. But he didn't stay. And it was funny. After all that wanting him to come home, I hated it when he was there. All that arguing and butting into the way Mum and I did things. So finally he went away and didn't come home again. And now he's married to somebody else. And sometimes I forget all about him. But I don't, really."

Jessica felt hollow. "But, Margaret, does that mean it just gets worse and worse? When we grow up, will just more and more sad things happen to us? Then it's just like growing up is like going bad. Then why bother going to school? Why bother having babies? They just die." She dropped Margaret's hand, jumped up and launched herself onto the bed, pushing her face into the cover.

The soft roar of conversation and the clink of teacups floated up from downstairs. Jessica breathed in through the covers—hot, damp, and slightly dusty air. The bed jiggled as Margaret climbed onto the pillow end. "I don't think it gets worse and worse. I think it just gets to be more of a . . . sort of mixture, with different kinds of happy and sad. Anyway, when you're grown-up it seems like you get to make more things happen, not like when you're a kid and things just happen *to* you."

Jessica sat up. "I think things happen *to* everybody."

"Yeah, maybe. But when I finish being a kid I'm going to make lots of things happen." Margaret bounced up and down so hard that the headboard began to tap against the wall. "Hey, Jess?"

"Yeah."

"You have bedspread marks all over your face."

Something rose in Jessica's throat, a giggle or a sob, and she began to rub her cheeks. Mum called from the bottom of the stairs, "Margaret! Your mother's leaving."

Margaret jumped off the bed. "Better go."

"Okay. Margaret?"

"Yeah."

"I'm sorry about your dad."

Margaret gave a short nod and then threw a pillow at Jessica. "See you soon, baboon."

11

*A*untie Eileen decided to stay for a while after the funeral. At dinner she filled in the silences. "I was in the post office today and there was this woman trying to mail a big parcel to somewhere in Europe. She wanted to register it, I think. But she didn't speak English very well and the post office guy was just being *revolting*, saying, 'I don't understand you, ma'am' in that totally unhelpful way. You know who he reminded me of, Susan? Fish-Face Watson. Remember old Fish-Face?"

Mum smiled and nodded. Jessica perked up. Oh, good. A Baba story. Baba was Mum and Eileen's mother. She had died before Jessica was born and Mum didn't talk about her much. So Jessica was glad when Auntie Eileen told stories. She figured that Baba must have been a bit like Margaret—cheeky, brave, and fun. She had worked in a lamp factory, painting the bases of lamps with scenes of white-wigged people on swings and ruined castles and Spanish ladies with flowers in their hair.

At the foot of her bed, Jessica had a little painting that Baba had done. It was very dark, of two roses in a vase. The white one was standing up and the red one was drooping. Through half-shut eyes or in the dim light, Jessica always made it into a picture of an elephant.

Jessica loved the stories about how Baba didn't want Mum to marry Dad, stories she would never have found out if it hadn't been for Auntie Eileen.

". . . yeah, old Fish-Face." Auntie Eileen looked at Simon and Jessica. "He was Baba's boss at the lamp factory. Did I ever tell you about the time Baba got everyone to threaten to quit just before Christmas?"

Jessica settled back for the familiar story that was as comfortable as an old pair of jeans. She remembered that it had something to do with Baba organizing a union and being a hero. But in the pause while Auntie Eileen sipped her wine, Simon mumbled, "Only about a million times."

There was a long moment of shocked silence. Then Jessica heard two sounds, the scrape of Mum's chair and a wham as Mum grabbed Simon by his jacket and slammed him against the wall. She ripped off his headphones and threw them on the floor.

"I've had it with you, Simon. You're acting like a jerk. Apologize to Eileen right now."

"Susan, *Susan*, It's all right. I know Simon didn't mean to be rude."

Simon turned very pale. Then he pushed Mum away and said in a low voice, "Fuck off. Just leave me *alone*." The front door slammed behind him.

Jessica heard a roaring in her ears. She looked down at the pattern on her fork. Mum sat down as though nothing was wrong and picked up her spoon to eat her strawberries. But the spoon rattled against the glass bowl and then Mum's head was on the table and she began to make a gulping sort of noise.

Auntie Eileen held her hand out to Jessica. "Come on, kiddo."

One of the traditions of a visit from Auntie Eileen was the walk to the drugstore. So when they left the house, they naturally headed that way. When they arrived, Auntie Eileen said the same thing as always. "The sky's the limit, kiddo." That meant that she would buy Jessica one thing, whatever she wanted. Once it had been a pink satin pig with wings. One year it had been a make-your-own-jewelry kit. Some choices had been better than others. The little sponges that were supposed to turn into animals when you put them in water just turned into soggy blobs. But the crystal garden was great. Jessica had kept it until it got dusty.

In the last couple of years, Jessica had headed straight for the stationery aisle. But this time everything on the shelves looked, well, just like more stuff. Stuff that you kept until it was used up or wrecked. Stuff that you kept until you were tired of it and then you threw it away.

Suddenly Jessica knew that she didn't want anything. There was nothing at all in the bright store that she wished for. She lined up her sneakers on the exact line of the tiles on the drugstore floor.

"So what's it to be this time?" Auntie Eileen wandered over from the best-sellers.

Jessica knew if she said she didn't want anything, it would either sound sulky or else it would sound like she was whining for attention. So she reached out blindly and picked a package of metallic outline pens.

When they arrived home, Mum had gone to bed and Simon was still out. Dad was watching TV. Or at least the TV was on and Dad was sitting in front of it. Jessica sat at the kitchen table and doodled with her new pens for a while, until she felt tiredness come down over her like a big thick blanket. When Simon crashed onto the air mattress much later, she barely woke up.

The next day Mum didn't get out of bed in the morning. "Mum is not feeling well today," said Dad. He spent hours in their room and Jessica could hear talking, but mostly Dad's voice, not Mum's.

Jessica spent the morning making a picture with her new pens. It was a circus scene. In the bottom part was a dancing bear. He turned out very bulgy and a bit sad. On the top was a beautiful trapeze artist wearing a spangly purple dress and hanging from her knees. Her hands were extended. She was about to fly through the air to be caught. Whoever was reaching for her hands wasn't in the picture. For background, Jessica penciled in faces for the audience, just circles with eyes. Some were looking down to the bear, some up to the trapeze lady.

When Mum got up at noon, Jessica gave her the picture. But Mum looked at it as though she didn't know what it was and said, "This is lovely. Thank you." She sounded like she was reading the line from a cue card at the Academy Awards, or like she didn't speak English very often. What was wrong with Mum? Why was she acting so weird? Dad had to keep telling her what to do. "Have a cup of tea now, Susan."

For lunch Dad heated up canned soup. He didn't even add parsley or croutons. Jessica could never remember Dad cooking such a plain lunch. Mum didn't eat any. A few guitar chords floated up from the basement. Jessica looked at Mum to share the joke, but she was just looking into space. The air in the room was getting heavier and heavier.

"Dad, don't we need something from the store?"

Dad was just starting to say, "No," when he looked over at Jessica's face. "Sure," he replied. "Go along and get us some apple juice, would you? Olafson's is a good place for that."

Olafson's was farther away than the usual store and

Jessica knew they had exactly the same apple juice everywhere. When Dad handed her the money, he gave her hand a good squeeze.

When Jessica returned, Mum had gone back to bed. It didn't make any sense. Was Mum sick? But she was suddenly too tired to ask. She was tried of trying to figure things out. She was tired of looking inside.

The next few days passed in a fog. Mum wasn't really there. Sometimes Jessica caught her mother looking at her in a frightened way. And Dad never lost his faraway look. Simon was very quiet or else out. Rowan dropped in. Auntie Eileen tried to do all the ordinary things like washing and meals and conversation.

Jessica mooched around and tried to ignore the complicated hurt inside her. When Lucie had just died, the hurt was big but plain. Every part of her had felt the same, just wanting Lucie to be alive again. But now none of the parts seemed to go together.

She felt twitchy. She did not feel like a good person. She was lonely but she didn't want to see anyone, even Margaret. She was sad but she couldn't cry, angry but she couldn't yell. She was frightened but she couldn't pull the covers over her head or sit up straight and shout, "Boo!" And she couldn't see what the end would be.

12

"Nancy waved a cheery goodbye to slim, handsome Ned Nickerson, hopped into her red roadster and she and plump, pretty Bess Marvin roared off towards the mysterious Gladiola Grotto."

Jessica's elbows were digging little holes in the carpet, so she rolled over onto her back, held the book above her head at arm's length and reread the sentence, tasting the word "grotto." The cave scene was coming up. Little did Nancy and Bess know that they would lose their way and then be held prisoner by the diamond smugglers. Bess would go all to pieces, but luckily Nancy had left a note in code for tomboy George. Jessica could recall the plot perfectly because she had read *Secret of the Grotto* only the week before. In fourth grade, she and Margaret had decided that Nancy Drew books were boring and dumb, so Jessica's collection had been in a box under her bed.

But these days it seemed like the only happy place in the world was River Heights and the only person you could count on was Nancy. Jessica was on her second re-read of the entire collection. She was up to four Nancy Drews a day. She squirmed around until the afternoon sun, shining into her bedroom, hit the pages of the book. Summer sounds filtered into her room—the rasp of the lawn mower, the neighbor's opera broadcast, a garbage truck in the alley. But none of it was as real as the roar of the roadster, Bess's tinkling laugh, and George's hearty chuckle.

But then one real-life noise cut in. It was Charlene's moped, popping down the side path.

Since Lucie's death, there had been a terrible shyness between Jessica and Charlene. Charlene looked at Jessica as though she was scared or something. And Jessica didn't know how to *be* with Charlene. It seemed as though it would be disloyal to Lucie to go down to the basement and gossip about the soap operas. But more than anything, at this moment, Jessica wanted to.

She plunked her book on the floor and looked out the window down onto Charlene's head. It looked very strange to see a motorcycle helmet from above. It made Charlene look like some insect. Jessica started to call out hello. But then, just as Charlene opened her door, she took off her helmet and Jessica's stomach lurched. What was Charlene wearing on her head? Some kind of stocking? Why did her head look so small? It was almost as if Charlene had . . . no hair! Jessica went down to investigate.

When Charlene answered the door, Jessica couldn't think of a thing to say. She felt as though she had been transported into a science-fiction movie. Nobody had ever looked so different! The face was Charlene's, all right, but her head was completely bald. No hair at all. Charlene looked barely human.

"So, hi, Jess. Come on in."

"Charlene. What did you do?"

"Shaved my head. Like it?"

Jessica didn't have time to be polite. "NO!"

Charlene grinned. "Well, you're with everyone else. Nobody likes it except me."

"Why did you do it?"

"It's a long story. Come on in."

Jessica settled down on Charlene's futon with a can of Coke. Drops of condensation fell onto her bare knees.

". . . so I said, 'Yes, Diane, I really mean it. I want you to shave my head.' Well, you can imagine what the other people in the shop thought. Mrs. Salter, you know the one with the cockapoos that peed on the floor when she was having her perm? Well, she was in for her Saturday wash and set. When she put her glasses on, she just about lost her dentures."

"But why *did* you? It looks so weird."

"For one thing, don't you ever wonder what your head

looks like? I mean, really, the shape of it and all? I mean, here we could go through life never knowing what our scalps look like. I wanted to see."

"I've never once wondered that. I don't like to think about my insides."

"But aren't you curious? I sure am. If I ever had an operation where they cut me open, I'd make them keep me awake so I could look. I mean, it's *my* inside after all."

Jessica tried to feel herself from the outside in. Skin. What next? Her stomach was certainly there, all knotted up at the moment. What else? A bit of an ache in the back from lying on the floor reading. Heart beating. Ribs, having to go to the bathroom, being a bit full. Jessica felt her fingers go hollow. "Yuck."

"But haven't you ever seen an X-ray of yourself?"

"Yeah, when I broke my wrist. But it was sort of blurry, not like a skeleton costume."

"Anyway, back to scalps. In the olden days, people were really interested in the shape of skulls. There was even this goofy science about it. They thought you could tell a lot about a person's personality from the lumps they had on their head. Like, if you had this particular lump called the 'bump of locality,' then you were good at directions. Stuff like that."

"But it looks terrible."

"Yeah, I know. But that's just because we're not used to it. Anyway, it keeps them from going to sleep at the shop."

"So what's new at the shop?"

Jessica floated along on the wave of Charlene's voice. How Julius who owned the store was going to enter the triathalon and about how he discussed swimming all the time and how his wife, Maureen, told Julius she would leave him if he mentioned free-style technique one more time and how Julius thought she should be grateful that he was taking care of himself and not letting himself go, like some people he could mention, and how Maureen got really mad and threw Julius's running shoes out the apartment window into the dumpster and how when Julius went to get them they were covered in rotting garbage.

Then the soaps came on TV and Charlene had to talk a lot through them because Jessica had lost track. All the Coke and laughing made Jessica definitely have to use the toilet. On her way back to the TV, she passed behind the couch where Charlene was sitting. Suddenly she just had to feel Charlene's head. Her hand did it before she thought about it. The skin felt very thin and slightly fuzzy. The bone was right there. Charlene gave a little jump and Jessica was embarrassed.

"Oh, I'm sorry. I just, well, I just wanted to know what a skull felt like."

"No, that's okay. Everybody is curious. Want to feel the very strangest thing?" Charlene guided Jessica's hand to the back of the shaved head. "There's a kind of a flat spot here. Do you think I was born that way, or is it from sleeping on it? I figure it could be from sleeping on it.

Have you ever seen that display at the museum? They've got this Haida skull. They used to strap boards to their foreheads to flatten them. We should go some day . . ."

Suddenly Jessica's hand sparked a memory. What was this like? Oh, yes. It was like touching Lucie's head. Jessica took the thought and tried to throw it away. But it boomeranged back. She let her hand fall. Here she was, laughing and happy and having a good time. She had forgotten.

". . . yeah, we could go down to the museum some Sunday and have brunch and then we could go to the display . . . Hey, Jess, what's wrong?"

"Nothing." Jessica headed blindly towards the door. "Gotta go."

"Oh. Okay. Bye."

Jessica made it to the forsythia bush by the back fence before a sob escaped her. She crawled in under its hanging branches. Her hideout. She leaned against the fence and took a deep, unsteady breath. She didn't cry. She rested her chin on her rough knees and moved her head back and forth, liking the scratchiness. Then she hugged herself as hard as she could, squishing her body into as small a space as possible. Maybe she could squish herself together like a lump of plasticene and just roll away. Her mind was just rolling herself out the front gate when she heard Charlene's door open.

"Jess. Jessica!"

Jessica stayed very quiet. The door snicked shut again.

Jessica felt her chest rise and fall against her legs. Her nose began to drip. She sat up to reach into her shorts pocket and her head hit a branch of the shrub. She'd grown too big for the hideout. She would have had to tell Lucie about it. Now Jessica really needed a Kleenex but her pockets were empty. Her neck was starting to hurt from being cramped. He feet took her back to Charlene's door.

"Char. I need a Kleenex."

"Oh, so do I." Charlene didn't have any so they shared a roll of toilet paper.

"Char. We never talk about Lucie." Jessica pushed the words out of her tight throat.

"Oh, Jessie. I thought you didn't want to. Like when we were talking about X-rays, I wanted to say how great that ultrasound scan thing must have been for your mum and dad before Lucie was born. But I didn't think I should. I thought it would make you too sad."

"I'm sad anyway."

"I'm so sorry. I just didn't know what to say. I've never known anyone who . . . who died before. I needed someone to talk to but then I thought, well, I shouldn't talk to *you* because she wasn't my sister. I couldn't be sad like you're sad. And anyway it would be selfish because I needed to talk to you not to cheer *you* up but to cheer *me* up. I mean, you have your whole family."

Jessica thought about Mum's empty eyes. It was too big to tell Charlene.

"Char?" Charlene nodded. "I missed coming down to visit you."

"I missed you, too. It's fun when you come." In the silence the TV blatted on.

"But, Char, I feel bad about having fun. I feel really mean when I laugh and Lucie's dead."

Charlene reached up her hand to run her fingers through her hair, encountered nothing, and gave Jessica a weak grin. "Well, here's what I figure. You had lots of fun with Lucie, right?" Jessica nodded. "Then one way of keeping part of Lucie alive is to keep that feeling, to remember it."

Jessica held the thought for a moment and felt a slight cool breeze blow through her mind. Put like that it sounded like there might be some sense to it. She stored the thought away to look at later and switched her attention to the TV.

Charlene wouldn't mind if she didn't say anything for a while.

13

*S*aturday morning Dad announced that it was clean-up time. Jessica was relieved. Saturday morning was always clean-up time.

"Surfaces," Mum used to say. "Once a week I want to see surfaces." So on Saturday mornings they all had a job. This had been the subject of a long family meeting. The only thing Simon would do was wash the car.

"What can you do?" said Dad. "Give them alternative role models and still the only thing they'll do is wash the car."

Jessica picked the upstairs bathroom. She liked bathroom duty because it was quiet. You could listen to the radio, not like vacuuming. And after the real work of washing the floor or cleaning the tub, it was fun to arrange the towels, to mix and match the colors.

Jessica did an extra-special job this time, putting the bathmat in the wash, wiping down the shelves in the medicine cabinet, throwing out the magazines that had been dropped in the bath and picking new ones for the magazine rack, folding the end of the toilet paper like in a motel. But even then it didn't take much time. Auntie Eileen must have been cleaning.

Jessica ran downstairs with a bag of wastepaper and swung around the banister. Mum was in the living room dusting the coffee table. In the kitchen, Dad had the hair dryer in one hand and a chopstick in the other as he defrosted the fridge. "Defrost your freezer in just thirty minutes using the patent blow-dry Chinese food technique. Not available in stores. Write now for an exclusive catalogue."

Jessica giggled and grabbed an apple and sat up on the kitchen counter. "Hey, Dad, what's another name for chicken?"

"Don't know."

"Tuna of the land. Get it? Chicken of the sea, tuna of the land."

Dad turned around and gave Jessica a blast from the hair dryer. "That's good. What's another one? I know. What can you call a ship?" Jessica shook her head. "Camel of the ocean. Like—camels are the ships of the desert. We should try to make some money on this kind of joke. But I don't know what we'd call it."

Jessica heard the washing machine stop and remembered the wet towels she had left on the bathroom floor.

As she passed through the living room, she saw Mum still dusting the coffee table. She paused on the landing. Mum moved a pile of books to one end of the table and dusted one half. Then she moved the books back and dusted the other half. But as Jessica watched, she saw Mum move the same books back and forth three times. The small piece of happiness that Dad's fooling had given her was burnt up.

She wanted to scream, "Stop acting like some retard. Stop dusting. You've done that already. Don't be so *stupid*. Pay attention. Wake up. Come back." But she didn't scream anything. Instead she went upstairs to her room and closed the door.

She sat at her desk. She doodled with her felt-tip markers. She tested how hard she could pretend to staple her finger before it really hurt. She ran her hand across the smooth wood of the desk and remembered the night befor her eleventh birthday, last January, a million years ago.

She had been made to sleep in Lavinia's room on the air mattress, because in the morning her present was going to be in her room. When she saw it, she thought she could never be happier. The little flip-top desk was wrapped up in a big blue ribbon and it glowed like sunshine. It had brass pulls and hinges, and a shelf on top, and a shelf on the bottom. On the top shelf was a glass marmalade jar with three new pencils and a fountain pen. On the bottom shelf were a desk encyclopedia and a grown-up dictionary.

But the best part was when you pulled down the front

of the desk to make a top to write on. Inside were little drawers and cubbyholes. Each had something in it. There were sheets of thick writing paper and two sizes of envelopes, a stapler, and a staple remover. Two kinds of tape, magic and regular. A pair of scissors with bright blue handles. A bottle of white-out. A glue stick. Paper clips, staples, and thumbtacks. The big drawer had seven file folders in it, one for each color of the rainbow. The drawer had a key.

In the very last tiny drawer was a card: "Dad found it. Rowan stripped and oiled it. Auntie Eileen and Simon found the things to go in it. Mum bought the books."

Jessica opened the big drawer and took out "The Baby Project." She removed it from its folder and carefully put the folder away. Then she took her scissors and cut through the first page. Corner to corner. The second page she cut into long thin strips. The third she cut around in a spiral. The fourth she ripped into confetti. The fifth she folded as many times as she could. The rest of the pages she scrunched up and stuffed into her wastepaper basket. Then she began to sharpen all her pencils.

"Jessica, can you finish up in the bathroom?" Jessica didn't answer. Dad knocked and came in. "Hey, Jess, there's a bunch of soggy towels that should go in the next wash."

Jessica didn't turn around. The only answer was the rustling of paper in the wastebasket as some of the scrunched paper unscrunched. Dad leaned over and pulled one out. "Oh, Jessie." He put his hand on her shoulder.

It felt very heavy. Go away, said Jessica to herself and shrugged off Dad's hand. Dad began to talk. His voice was funny, tight and small.

"Jessie, I . . ." Jessica talked loud inside her head. "I'm not listening. I'm not listening. One for the money, two for the road, three to get ready, and four to go. TWO FOUR SIX EIGHT WHO DO WE APPRECIATE. ONE TWO THREE FOUR FIVE, ONCE I CAUGHT A FISH ALIVE, SIX SEVEN EIGHT NINE TEN, THEN I THREW HIM BACK AGAIN."

". . . so would you be able to come and help?"

The inside voice flicked off. "Help with what?"

"Crabbing," said Dad. "I thought I would go out to the pier this afternoon and try to get some crabs for dinner. Want to come? I could use the extra pair of hands." Jessica just nodded.

The pier wasn't crowded. Everyone was down at the organized end of the beach, lying on towels, playing radios or volleyball, windsurfing. There were only two men with crab traps in the water. Jessica peeked into their buckets. Empty.

"Not so good for crabs today," one said cheerfully. "Look why." He pointed out to the ocean. Sure enough, there was the small doggy head of a seal.

"Too much competition," said Dad with a grin. He unwrapped the chicken backs and necks and wired them to the bottom of the traps. Jessica used the proper metal trap and Dad used the homemade bicycle wheel and fishnet invention. They tied the end of their long yellow ropes to some staples in the pier and then swung the traps out into the water, letting the line run between their fingers. Jessica got a rope burn, as usual.

Then they settled down to wait. Crabbing was mostly waiting. Jessica lay on her stomach and looked down into the water.

"You must have been pretty mad to cut up 'The Baby Project.' You worked hard on it."

Jessica let her head flop over the end of the pier. "I was."

"Who were you mad at?"

"Mum."

"Do you want to talk about why?"

Suddenly Jessica sat up. "Dad, what's the matter with her?"

"I think she's feeling so sad that she can't manage ordinary things for a while."

"But you're sad and you're not acting, you know, stupid."

"I know, but something different has happened to Mum. She's used to always being strong and solving things, so when she can't it's even harder for her."

"I don't get it."

"Well, it's sort of like cooking. Like Mum has forgotten all her recipes. You know how it's a lot easier to use a recipe if it comes with a picture? Then you know what you're working towards. You can make little decisions along the way, how brown to sauté the onions, what size to dice the green peppers, because you know what you are heading towards. With recipes that have no picture, you have to make one up in your mind. Usually, of course, for everyday cooking you don't have a picture or a recipe, either. You just do it automatically."

The seal came nearer and gave a little strangled bark, but Dad didn't notice. "Mostly we go through life like that. We can make little decisions like what shoes to wear in the morning or big decisions like having a baby, because in the back of our heads we have a picture of what it all adds up to. I think what's happening to Mum at the moment is that the picture has disappeared. So she knows she has to get up, get dressed, talk on the telephone, but she can't make any decisions because she doesn't know what the end product is going to be. She can't see the point of things. Because Lucie's death didn't make any sense, none of the other things in life make any sense to her right now."

"It didn't make any sense to me, either," Jessica said quietly.

"I know, Jess, and that's where we're all different. You know how after the funeral you ate everything in sight and Simon didn't want to eat at all? Grief just takes people in different ways. For me it's a big help to just keep on doing things, to keep following the instructions in the recipe. We each have to find our own way."

Part of this made no sense to Jessica. It didn't seem as if Dad was really answering her question.

"Time to check the traps," said Dad. They heaved them up out of the water, hand over hand. Dad's was completely empty and the chicken was a bit chewed. Jessica's had a baby crab in it. Dad pulled it off carefully and threw it back in the water. As they swung the traps back and forth before throwing them in again, drops of water sprayed out from them, dotting the pier.

"Come on, guys," said Dad. "Kentucky Fried, just for you."

"Dad?"

"Yes."

"Is Mum ever going to get her picture back?"

"Yes, she is, for sure. She's already improving. She's strong. Not just on the surface, but all the way through." Dad looked out across the bay.

"Promise?"

"Promise what?"

"Promise that Mum will get better." Jessica grabbed Dad's arm and squeezed. He covered her hand with his.

"Yes, I promise. It'll take some time and we all have to help each other, but . . . yes."

14

A few weeks passed. With August had come the heat they had all longed for during the whole of cool, rainy June and July. Heat for turning your pillow over to the cool side and sitting on the front porch at night. The tomatoes finally had started to ripen. Margaret had gone away to camp.

Dad drove his taxi off and on. Charlene let her hair grow and started to look like a hedgehog. Auntie Eileen booked her flight to Toronto. The drugstore got in its school supplies.

Mum started to work at home again. Jessica heard the blip and peep of Lavinia coming from the office. One day she wandered in and Mum explained what she was doing. Late at night when it was too hot to sleep, they began to work on a program to play cribbage. Mum stopped looking so frightened. Sometimes she even talked in capitals again.

Simon spent most of his time hanging out with Patrick and the rest of the time watching TV. He didn't wear his Walkman to meals but he might as well have for all the talking he did. Jessica was usually asleep when he came in at night. But one night he stubbed his toe on the dresser and woke her up. She didn't move.

She heard him blowing up the air mattress with the pump. *Shhh-pop. Shhh-pop.* The sound reminded her of their camping trip last summer. Dad had taken the two of them on a holiday. Mum had stayed home with "the big lovely empty house and Lavinia." It had been just for the long weekend and it had rained every minute. The tent had begun to smell like chicken-in-a-mug. Simon had ignored the rain and gone swimming and canoeing and tried to build fires with wet kindling. Jessica had read all her books three times and played the recorder.

Last summer. Lucie hadn't died then. Lucie hadn't been born then. Lucie hadn't even—Jessica counted up on her fingers—been started. She hadn't existed at all and now she didn't again.

Jessica heard Simon settle into his sleeping bag. Suddenly she absolutely had to be on her stomach. But if Simon knew she was awake, he would wonder why she hadn't said anything. The silence was crackling.

"Sime?" It came out like a blurt into the silence and darkness of the bedroom.

The shifting and snuffling stopped. "Yeah?"

Jessica needed something to say where the words didn't matter. "Sime, what's tough?"

There was a pause. "Life's tough."

"What's life?"

"Life's a magazine."

"How much does it cost?"

"Twenty-five cents."

"I've only got a dime."

"That's tough."

"What's tough."

Silence again, but this time it was a warm, listening silence. Jessica heard Simon shuffle up to a sitting position. "Hey, Jess, you know this heredity stuff?"

"Yes."

"Well, you know, we never did know what color Lucie's eyes were going to be for sure, did we?"

Jessica had never understood "burst into tears" before. But one beat after Simon's words, she was crying with every part of her. Simon waited until the worst was over and then she saw the black shape of his arm stretch over the side of the bed. His hand was full of Kleenex. Jessica needed them all. Her whole face was wet, even the insides of her ears.

"Jess, are you sleepy?"

"No."

"Then get up. I have an idea. Get dressed but be very quiet and don't turn the light on. I'm going on reconnaissance, but I'll be back in a minute." Simon left, shutting the door very quietly behind him.

By the time he got back, Jessica was dressed and sitting on the edge of her bed in the dark.

"All clear. Come on."

"But where are we going?"

"Shhhh. Just follow me."

In the front hall, oddly lit by the streetlight, they grabbed their jackets. Then out the front door and down the side path to the shed. Simon wheeled two bikes out and pushed one over to Jessica. "Care for a spin?"

"Simon, I don't think we should. What if Mum and Dad wake up and find us gone? They'll be worried. I don't think we should do something bad. I mean, you're in enough trouble already."

Simon gave his bike a jerk. "It's three o'clock in the morning. They'll never know. But even if they do and we get heck, that's just what happens in families. It's normal. NORMAL. Not like babies dying. So are you coming or not?" He flipped his leg over the crossbar and rode up the drive.

Jessica jumped on her banana seat and followed.

There was a faint edge of light to the sky and everything felt new and unfamiliar. The soft air cooled Jessica's red eyes. The buildings looked like the cutout skyline at the planetarium show.

Jessica and Simon freewheeled down the hill toward the beach. Simon put on a burst of speed and reached the bottom, turned and pumped his way back to Jessica, riding circles around her. When they reached the bridge there wasn't a single car on it, so they rode up the middle of the center lane. At the top they stopped. The freighters were big dark shapes out in the bay.

"Have you ever seen the bridge this empty?" said Jessica.

"Just when the Queen came to visit," said Simon, and he gave one big push and began to coast down the other side, no hands, waving the Queen's windshield-wiper wave, first on one side and then the other.

"And I'm the motorcycle escort," yelled Jessica, whizzing past him with loud vrooming noises. As they rounded the curve to follow the beach road, a police car passed them going onto the bridge. Jessica felt scared and expected a flashing light any minute. "Phew," she exclaimed, as the car carried on its way. And then she realized that there wasn't anything wrong with what they were doing. All night, every night as she lay sleeping and dreaming, there was this same and different world and she had never seen it before.

In the long and rhythmical pedal around the beach walk, Jessica stopped thinking. Her mind was in her legs. Push and relax, push and relax, push and coast. The tight place in her began to dissolve. The sky lightened and the breeze died down. The streetlights flicked off. Only police cars and taxis and newspaper delivery vans were on the road. Her handle grips dug ridges into her hands.

Simon gave a big, extravagant right-hand turn signal, and soon they were back on city streets. They met a paper boy and exchanged big waves. They wheeled past high apartments with only a sprinkling of lights on. Bakers just home from work? People watching the late-late show? Or . . . and Jessica let herself think it before she could stop herself . . . somebody with a baby, feeding it, or walking with it to stop it crying?

It was uphill now and Jessica welcomed the hard push it took to make it to the top. Her question was in the rhythm of her legs:

why
did
she
die
why
did
she
die.

They rode up the downtown mall. It was quiet even there. A few bundles of rags in doorways were people, Jessica knew. But how different it was from when you walked there after a movie, when it was frightening and loud and neon. Now there was even a dog, nosing around the garbage cans. At the top of the mall, Simon pulled up outside of Denny's. "Care for a coffee?"

They leaned their bikes against the window and walked in under the big pink and orange "We Never Close" sign. There was just one tough-looking man sitting at the counter, smoking. The waitress must have been lonely, because she bounced right over and was very friendly.

"Hi, there. My name's Barbara and I'm your waitress. Of course I'm your waitress. What else would I be? Silly thing to say, really. Anyway, what can I getcha?"

"Two hot chocolates, please," said Simon.

"Whipped cream with that?" They both nodded.

"You got it." Barbara bellowed into the kitchen "Double hoe-choes, Larry. Whipped moo. Snap it up."

Simon ate his whipped cream off the top and got it all over his nose. Jessica stirred hers in. "Sime?"

"Yeah."

"Have you used the microphone on your tape recorder lately?"

"Yeah, why?"

"Did it work?"

"It works okay. It's not a great machine, you know."

"Did it always work?"

"Sure. Oh, come to think of it, a while ago I noticed that the batteries were in upside down. It worked okay when I fixed them. What's up, anyway? You want to borrow it?"

So in between sips of chocolate, Jessica told Simon the whole story of the baby tape. Simon started to laugh. "You attached it to the sponge mop? Margaret did what?" Barbara gave up pretending not to listen and sat down at the booth with them. The tough guy looked disgusted and left.

Soon they were all laughing so hard that Larry, a skinny bald man in a greasy apron, came out of the kitchen and they had to tell it again.

"It all started when I decided to make a tape of the waves to help my baby sister sleep . . ."

When they finished Barbara pulled their bill off her waitress pad and tore it up. "This is on me, kids."

"Oh, no," said Simon, standing up, "I insist." And he reached into his pack and pulled out six purple rolls of pennies. He lined them up on the counter. "Keep the change."

"You guys," said Barbara. "You're choice. Larry, aren't these guys choice? Hey, come again, eh?"

They rode slowly up the bridge on the way home and coasted down in lazy loops. They stopped by the drinking fountain at the concession stand before the final short hill to home. Jessica let the cold water run in and out of her mouth, washing away the thick sweet taste of chocolate. Then she turned her face this way and that, wetting her nose and cheeks and eyes. She dried her face on her jacket. She looked at her watch: 5:32. A faint full roar of traffic was beginning. Suddenly her legs began to tremble. She was very, very tired.

"Let's do this again," said Simon. "Let's do it when I'm thirty and you're . . ." he paused, "twenty-seven. Let's do it on my thirtieth birthday."

"We won't," said Jessica. "We'll forget or we'll think it's silly or we won't live in the same place."

Simon's face got very still. "We *will* do it." He stuck his chin out. "Wherever I am, I'll fly to wherever you are for my thirtieth birthday. I swear it now. It's a pact." He hunted in his various pockets until he found a safety pin. "Promise in blood," he said and pricked his finger. Jessica took the pin and did the same and they held their fingers together for a minute. Then Jessica popped hers into her mouth.

They walked their bikes home up the last hill. On the way up the stairs, Simon tripped and Jessica gave a loud "Shhh" and Simon doubled over trying not to laugh and walked headfirst into the hall telephone table. Mum came out in her dressing gown. "What the . . . ? Where . . . ?"

Jessica felt Simon stiffen beside her. But then Mum took one look at their faces and smiled. "This has the makings of a long story. Let's save it." Then she gave them each a shoulder squeeze. "Time for bed or back to bed or whatever."

Simon headed for the bathroom. Jessica left her clothes in a tangled heap on the floor and slid into her unmade bed. She fell asleep to the hiss of the shower.